DOUBLE PHOENIX

THE FIREBIRD	FROM THE WORLD'S END
Edmund Cooper	Roger Lancelyn Green

Introduction by
LIN CARTER

BALLANTINE BOOKS • NEW YORK
An Intext Publisher

Introduction Copyright © 1971 by Lin Carter

THE FIREBIRD Copyright © 1971 by Edmund Cooper

FROM THE WORLD'S END Copyright © 1948
by Roger Lancelyn Green. First published in England
by Edmund Ward

SBN 345-02420-6-125

First Printing: November, 1971

Printed in the United States of America

Cover art by Gervasio Gallardo

BALLANTINE BOOKS, INC.
101 Fifth Avenue, New York, N. Y. 10003

About THE FIREBIRD *and*
Edmund Cooper:

PHOENIX TIMES TWO

This latest volume in our Adult Fantasy Series is unique for two reasons. In the first place, it exists because of a remarkable coincidence; in the second, it attempts to revive a long-neglected and nearly extinct art form. First, about the coincidence.

Last year we received a manuscript from the British science fiction writer Edmund Cooper, several of whose early books had been published in the U.S.A. by Ballantine. The manuscript in question was a novella entitled *The Firebird*. Mrs. Ballantine read it and liked it. I read it and liked it. But the problem was *length:* at about thirty or thirty-five thousand words, *The Firebird* was far too short to appear as a book all by itself—about half as long as the average paperback novel.

Around the same time as I received Mr. Cooper's MS, I had begun correspondence with another British writer, Roger Lancelyn Green. A couple of readers of our Adult Fantasy Series had called to my attention a novel by Mr. Green called *From the World's End*. This book had been published a dozen or fifteen years previously by the firm of Edmund Ward in Leicester, but I had never read it and did not have a copy. I wrote to Roger Lancelyn Green, asking about the book, and received a charming letter of reply, as well as the author's own copy of *From the World's End*.

You may imagine my surprise and delight when I discovered that Mr. Green's book was not only the same *kind* of story as Mr. Cooper's—and we'll get to that topic in just a minute—but also about the same word length.

Two thirty-five-thousand-word novellas on the same general theme, in the same literary genre, written independently by two different authors from the same country, coming to my editorial attention in the same two weeks adds up to quite a coincidence!

Our story has a happy ending: both short novels were marvelously delightful reading, both were purchased, and both now appear together in this country for the first time.

As for the "long-neglected and nearly extinct art form," I refer to an old and venerable style of story telling called *allegory*. My dictionary defines allegory as: "The veiled presentation, in a figurative story, of a meaning metaphorically implied but not expressly stated . . . allegory is prolonged metaphor, in which a series of actions are symbolic of other actions."

I wonder if you, like myself, tend to wince away from any story bearing the deadly label of allegory. When I hear that term I usually think of what must be the dullest book I ever tried to read (John Bunyan's *The Pilgrim's Progress*), and of what must surely be my least favorite of all the world's epic (or epic-length) poems, Edmund Spenser's *The Faerie Queen,* which took me a solid year to read and which required stern discipline to finish. Allegory is something of a dirty word to modern readers, and not without good reason. When you are trying to tell two different stories on two different levels—the narrative or surface level, and the symbolic level underneath—

the general tendency is to skimp on the story in order to underscore the symbolism. This makes for simply dreadful story telling and dull reading.

For some reason though, many great and gifted writers have been excited by the possibilities of allegory and have written stories in the form; and not all of them have been as dull as *Pilgrim's Progress*. A lot of James Branch Cabell's best fantasies contain scenes or passages or entire sequences aptly described as allegorical; many of George MacDonald's finest fairy stories (such as "The Golden Key") are largely allegorical. Which simply suggests that in the hands of a brilliant narrative artist, allegory can sometimes be beautiful and pleasurable literature.

Both Edmund Cooper and Roger Lancelyn Green have, in the two novellas of this book, tried to revive this long-neglected art form and to give it life. In this attempt they have not skimped at all on narrative, but have richly embellished their stories with lavish color and dreamlike imagery, hinting at the hidden meanings beneath. I find both of these short novels more than worthy of publication because I can read them as *stories* first and foremost. Whether or not you care to search out the symbolism beneath the surface is up to you.

Edmund Cooper was born in 1926 in Marple, Cheshire, and was educated at Manchester Grammar School and Didsbury Training College, but claims, "I distinguished myself by being backward at school, collecting several scholarships, and continuing to remain backward." He left school at fifteen and worked as a laborer; at sixteen he became a civil servant; at seventeen he trained for the sea; at twenty he became a teacher; and shortly thereafter he began to write. I gather he was not very successful at any of his early endeavors, but at writing he became most successful indeed. He published fifty short stories before his first book appeared, and possesses what must be a record by having sold the same short story thirteen times in one year, including a sale of the film rights to Hollywood.

Ballantine published his first book, a novel called *Deadly Image,* in 1958 when he was thirty-two. It was swiftly followed by a volume of short stories entitled *Tomorrow's Gift,* and another science fiction novel called *Seed of Light* in 1959. Since then several more books—both novels and short story collections —have appeared in this country, such as *Transit* (1964), *All Fools' Day, A Far Sunset,* and *News From Elsewhere* (1969).

He and his family live in Sussex, and he describes his special interests as "chess, philosophy, and wine."

About FROM THE WORLD'S END *and*
Roger Lancelyn Green:

Roger Lancelyn Green was born in 1918 of an old English family. He lives in Poulton Hall, an ancient country house in Cheshire which has belonged to his family for several centuries, on an estate older still. He studied at Merton College, Oxford, where he took a degree in English Literature and received the degree of Bachelor of Letters, and where he became good friends with the late C. S. Lewis.

At various times he had been an actor, a schoolmaster, and a bookseller, and for about five years he was Deputy Librarian at Merton College. Now he lives quietly at his country home with his wife and three children, and devotes his time to writing.

For many years I have known of Roger Green through his many books, and I have often thought that it would be fun to know him, as our tastes in books and writers agree to a remarkable extent. For example, I am interested in the author of *Alice in Wonderland*—and Roger has written a couple of books about him, such as *Lewis Carroll* (1960), a Walck monograph. I regard *Peter Pan* as one of the best of all stories for children, and Roger not only wrote a book about the history of the play, *Fifty Years of 'Peter Pan'* (1954), but also another Walck monograph on its author. I have the most enormous affection for Andrew Lang's "Color Fairy Books," and in particular for his children's novel, *Prince Prigio,* and Roger has also written a book called *Andrew Lang* (1962).

The best of all of his many, many books, however, is an invaluable history of children's story writers called *Tellers of Tales,* first published by Edmund Ward in 1946. I suspect that others share my enthusiasm for this book; at any rate, it has been reprinted twice since its first publication. In that precious volume, Roger devotes chapters packed with biographical information and literary lore to many of my all-time favorite writers: Lewis Carroll, J. M. Barrie, Kenneth Grahame, H. Rider Haggard, Andrew Lang, Hugh Lofting, E. Nesbit, George MacDonald, A. A. Milne, J. R. R. Tolkien, T. H. White, and C. S. Lewis, among others.

While I have long been familiar with Roger's scholarly nonfiction, I knew little about his own stories until he sent me *From the World's End.* Since then, we have exchanged many letters and he has sent me several of his books and also some unpublished manuscripts. So *From The World's End* is probably just the first work by Roger Lancelyn Green you will be seeing in the years to come under the Sign of the Unicorn's Head. . . .

About DOUBLE PHOENIX:

Perhaps the oddest of all the coincidences involved in the story behind this remarkable book is that both of our authors have used the symbol of the Phoenix—the fabulous "firebird of ancient poetic lore.

It was the old historian, Herodotus, who first wrote of this legendary creature. In *The Histories,* vol. II, 73, he records:

"There is another holy bird, called the Phœnix, which I have never seen but in pictures. He rarely appears in Egypt—only once in every five hundred years, so they say in Heliopolis—and he is supposed to come when his father dies. If the painters describe him truly, his plumage is part golden and part red, and he is very like an eagle in shape and size. They say that this bird comes from Arabia bringing the body of his father embalmed in myrrh to the Temple of the Sun, and there he buries him. First he moulds an egg of myrrh; then he puts his father in the middle of it; lastly he covers up the body with myrrh. This is what they say that this bird does. But I do not believe them."

Herodotus may have balked at accepting such a marvel, but later writers seized upon it with the creative enthusiasm of born fantasists and elaborated on the bare bones of the narrative above. Five centuries after Herodotus, the Roman historian Tacitus approved the Herodotian account, and touched it up slightly by setting the interval of the visits of the Phoenix to 1,461 years. (*Annals,* VI, 28.) Pliny, a bit later, tried to extend this figure to 12,994 years, but that was going a bit far even for Pliny. The poet Claudian, at the end of the fourth century, seems to have been the one who added the notion that the Phoenix, when near death, flies to the Temple of the Sun and immolates *himself* on a pyre of myrrh, rising reborn from his own ashes for another thousand years or so.

At any rate, a good idea only gets better in the retelling. Some of the people who have retold it have been Ovid (*Metamorphoses, XV*), Dante (*Inferno, XXIV*), and Milton, in his verse play, *Samson Agonistes*. Since the Phoenix is a marvelously apt symbol for the Christian myth of the resurrection of the flesh, it is no surprise to find early Christian apologists by the dozen listing the Phoenix either as a pagan symbol of the dogma, or even as *proof* of it —among them Tertulius, St. Ambrose, and Cyrillus of Jerusalem. More recently, the great Argentine writer, Jorge Luis Borges, discusses the legend of the Phoenix in his compendium, *The Book of Imaginary Beings* (New York: Dutton, 1969).

To this catalogue of famous writers may now be added the names of Edmund Cooper and Roger Lancelyn Green.

—LIN CARTER
Editorial Consultant:
The Ballantine Adult Fantasy Series

Hollis, Long Island, New York

The Firebird

The childhood shows the man,
As morning shows the day.
—*John Milton*

CONTENTS

A Green Cathedral

Dawn.

It was a world of strange shapes and shadows, impossible colours. It was a world of silence and beauty—a dark and dancing world still shivering under the flimsy mantle of light. It was an oyster shell opened to reveal the pearl of exceeding wonder. It was a ripple of music—a moment of sadness in the long and terrible laughter of life. It was the beginning.

On the rolling stillness of the land trees stood like tired soldiers, washed by the receding tides of mist. But there was no sound, or only the subtle whispers of a stillness before action; for all the hidden manoeuvres of the night were frozen by daybreak. And waiting lay heavily over the landscape, an invisible veil.

The house rose out of the mist, its mellow red bricks damp and shiny, its leaded windows glazed with a million drops of moisture. No smoke drifted from the chimneys, but tiny wisps of vapour hovered delicately upon lichen-daubed tiles as if their lazy movement mimicked the slow turning of the sleepers below.

The boy looked back at the house and thought of

his sleeping family. He was fond of them—as fond as one can be of strangers united only by blood and habit and love—but he had not told them of his intended departure. They would not have understood. They were too old—too old to imagine the shape of unimaginable journeys.

He stood a few paces from the door he had closed so softly behind him and gazed back at a house that had suddenly lost its meaning.

It was now no more than a chrysalis, a dead shell from which his spirit—his essential self—had crept like some bewildered imago.

Dominic was a strange child—strange as all children are until the light dies in their eyes and the fire goes out of their limbs and their strangeness is swallowed by cities and civilizations and the empty meaning of clocks. Dominic was a strange child, full of frightened courage and the urgency of forgotten dreams; full of death and immortality, and in love with both.

As he looked at the stillness of the house, he shivered, knowing that he would never enter it again. Dawn was a time of visions and decisions. They swirled about him as the mist swirled, plucking at his feet and fingers, creating in his eyes tears that he would never cry, and making his heart beat with hopes that might never be fulfilled.

But, whatever happened, he knew that he would not go back into the house again; knowing that footsteps can never be retraced, that every moment another moment dies, and that there are too many possibilities waiting to be born for any to have the gift of resurrection.

He did not need words for such thoughts. They were implicit in the transient dew on spiderwebs, the mist-hidden carpet of grass, the muted rustle of trees and the curdled fiery streaks along the eastern sky.

As the sun rose like a monstrous red balloon from distant pine trees, Dominic began to walk away. There was no sadness, only a sense of leaving.

Dominic half believed he would walk for ever through an eternal morning where mist drifted like a smoky ocean over the entire earth, where early sunlight sent fingers of day through a million cracks and openings in the trees' rooftops, and where stars faded on the ebb-tide of the west.

He was alone, but there was no sense of loneliness; for the morning had become a green cathedral as he walked among leaning columns of trees and watched the mist fight a slowly losing battle with the warmth of day. His thoughts were nowhere and everywhere as daylight whispered of hidden destinations and the blood in his veins sang of a thousand miracles that might imminently happen.

And presently one of them did.

The Thousandth Miracle

Dominic had reached a small clearing, not far from the lake, where the ruins of a derelict cottage—long rough-hewn beams, studded doors and broken pantiles—were returning to the earth from which they had long ago been drawn. It was a scene of enchantment; for here, obviously, were ghosts—invisible and friendly, bound for ever to a home that was itself a ghost.

Dominic surveyed the debris with pleasure and surprise. He realized that, though he might have passed by the ruined cottage before, he was seeing it for the first time.

The walls of the cottage had been reduced; but with odd persistence one doorway, complete with door, still remained standing. It was surrounded by rubble and ferns and the climbing luxuriance of honeysuckle. It was a green door set in a green world.

But, above all, it was a door that had to be opened. No one, thought Dominic as he scrambled over beams and broken window frames and the mounds of clay that had once been clean white walls, no one could possibly pass by such a door without opening it.

He gazed with delight at the rusty knocker. It was

a small iron hand loosely holding a massive ring. Below it, embedded in the door, lay the flattened striking piece, its face covered with a fine green cushion of moss. He lifted the ring and brought it down, but the moss muffled the sound of impact so that it could hardly be heard.

He tried again harder, but the bruised moss still held firm and the sound was swallowed. Dominic hammered on the door with his clenched hand; but the sound was no louder, and no one answered his summons.

He was disappointed. On such a morning such a door should have been opened. It was a time for mysteries and inexplicable happenings. A time for discovery.

Impulsively, he flung himself at the unresponsive door. It yielded easily—more easily than he had expected—and he half fell through the doorway on to what had once been a polished brick floor.

At the same time, his eyes were dazzled by an intense and shimmering light. In the moment that he stumbled he saw—he thought he saw—a bird of incredible plumage, a thing of fire and radiance, rise silently from the ruins to circle above his head.

There was no sound at all and yet—and yet the air was shaking with music; and there was such a nearness of beauty and power that the earth quivered beneath his feet; and there was the message of bells from a distant temple.

The boy shaded his eyes and glanced up. The looking brought pain—and ecstasy. There it hovered against trees and sky—a creature of flame whose wings made the very air dance with excitement.

Slowly, the Firebird circled over his head. Then, with slow wingbeats, it passed silently between the trees.

Dominic gazed spellbound after the bright majestic bird. He stood motionless, watching its fiery shape pass behind trees and over bushes—an unhurried flight that was neither a retreat nor an escape but a subtle invitation to follow.

In a single moment the boy's life had changed. He had opened a door to nowhere, not knowing that on the other side of the door the Firebird waited.

He rubbed his eyes and thought that he was dreaming. He rubbed his eyes again and knew that he was not dreaming. The reality of the Firebird was beyond doubt. The air was still alive with its memory: the derelict cottage was still somehow radiant with its passing.

Dominic knew that he would follow. He knew that there was nothing else to do but follow; for if he turned back through the doorway there would be nothing left for him but an ordinary world in which to live an ordinary life.

Here on the other side of the door, where the Firebird had been waiting, it was as if the world were in sharper focus—as if the air possessed a sudden tremendous clarity so that colours were brighter, contours sharper, and every leaf, every twig, every blade of grass of immense significance. It was as if the morning had been locked in crystal and the crystal bathed in light.

The boy's feelings suddenly changed to anxiety as he realized that the Firebird was already out of sight. He began to run, filled with a delicious fear that he had lost it—yet, at the same time, knowing that though he might never actually possess it neither would he ever completely lose it.

As he ran among the trees, Dominic caught another glimpse of the Firebird perhaps a hundred yards ahead in calm and unhurried flight. It hovered above a small colony of bramble bushes for a few moments—almost as if it were waiting for him—then it resumed its leisurely flight towards the lake.

The Golden Meteor

By the time Dominic had emerged from the long sprawling patch of trees, the Firebird was already skimming in graceful curves low over the still water. The heat from its wings annihilated the thin blanket of mist wherever it passed, describing hypnotic patterns which became themselves mobile, until it seemed as if the whole surface would soon be covered in fantastic tracery.

To Dominic the lake was more than a lake: it was a great inland sea with strange countries on the farther shore and still stranger mysteries on the island that rose almost in its geometrical centre and was oddly like the elbow of a submerged giant.

There was a building on the island. It looked like a tiny Greek temple with four scarred stone columns supporting a carved portico, and round the base were broad circular steps. It was, in fact, a disused folly that had been built in the days when such architectural extravagances were considered necessary to any civilized landscape. Much time had passed, however, since the laughter of cultured gentlemen, the delighted prattle of delicate ladies and other sounds of sylvan gaiety had echoed from it across the lake. Now its only occupants were insects and mosses, flowers and small wild creatures and the invisibly persistent shadows of things past.

Inside the folly there was a descending flight of steps leading originally to a semi-subterranean bower which was no doubt appropriate for the romantic foibles of an age of elegance. Dominic had been to the folly once before, but he had not ventured down the steps. He had no taste for grottoes that might house anything from a skeleton to an angry beast of darkness.

Now, as he stood at the edge of the lake, he saw that the Firebird, despite all its graceful digressions, was flying inevitably towards the island.

He remembered the boat he had used on the previous excursion and was relieved to see that it lay moored as he had left it by the broken-down wooden jetty—no more than a few planks on thin rotting piles—some fifty or sixty paces away. As he walked to the boat he began to think about the ruined cottage he had discovered, and wondered why he had not noticed it before. But perhaps it was simply because this was no ordinary morning. There was so much that he had already seen—and knew he would be seeing—for the first time.

He walked carefully along the loose planks to the boat, stepped carefully into it and cast off. The small rowing boat had settled a little on the mud of the lake bed; and he had to dig and push his way into free water with an old piece of weatherboard that did double duty as paddle and pole.

It was hard work getting away from the edge of the lake. By the time he was able to look up the Firebird was nowhere to be seen. Clearly, it had reached the island; for the heat of the rising sun had begun to disperse the mist and almost the whole expanse of water was now visible. With utter certainty, he knew that the Firebird had not passed the island or crossed to the other side of the lake, and he was vaguely puzzled by the sureness of his conviction.

Dominic began to paddle expertly and rhythmically with the old weatherboard so that the bows of the small boat pointed steadily at the distant target. Presently, the giant's elbow loomed large ahead of him; and as he paddled he both amused and frightened himself by trying to estimate the dimensions of the rest of the body that lay petrified beneath the surface of the water.

Presently, he was close enough to the island to see the tiny crevices in the stone columns of the folly and the flowers and weeds that had proudly allocated themselves a place in he sun along its waist-high, semi-circular parapet. But of the Firebird there was still no sign; and for the first time he began to have doubts—not so much of the Firebird's destination as of its very existence.

After all, there were such things as daydreams. Perhaps the Firebird was part of a daydream. Perhaps the dream was now ending. The thought seemed to cut like a knife; and he was filled with a dismal fear that the island would prove to be empty—empty of everything save the folly, a few stunted trees and the bitter mockery of ordinary, everyday birds.

But even as doubts assailed him, he found a reason for disproving reason. The Firebird could not belong to a daydream because a daydream would only be part of him, limited by his own thoughts and imaginings. Dominic knew that, alone, he would never have been able to dream of anything so beautiful, so full of power and purpose as a bird with fiery head and wings of flame, radiant as the sun yet gentle in movement, and of such splendour and such strange destiny that whoever followed it would surely understand the meaning of miracles.

As if in response to his thoughts, the Firebird suddenly rose from a patch of tall grasses and circled high over the boat while Dominic prepared to land. He gave a cry of delight and jumped ashore, pulling the boat after him as high as he could get it on the narrow border of mud and sandy earth. Meanwhile the Firebird spiralled higher and higher, its heat and radiance mingling with that of the morning sun, until it seemed to be no more than a burning point in the now clear sky.

The boy watched, fascinated and afraid. Was this to be the end of the journey, with the Firebird disappearing eventually into those high blue reaches and leaving only the memory of a brief pursuit that failed? He rejected the question even as he silently asked it. And it was as if he had signalled the Firebird's impossible return.

Down it came, a golden meteor. Down, down in a falling curve, and with such speed that its passage seemed to leave an arc of light carved briefly in the sky. Down to the disused folly it streaked to vanish behind the parapet in a moment of thunder and silence.

Dominic was appalled by the fierceness of that terrible dive. He gazed at the folly in an agony of suspense, half expecting some sign of the inevitable destruction. Surely the Firebird could only have dashed itself into a thousand fragments of light against the unyielding stone?

But there was no death glow, no explosive radiance, nothing. The folly continued to bask serenely and quietly in warm sunlight as if all were entirely normal on this most normal of mornings. Presently, movement returned to the boy's limbs and he went forward cautiously to explore.

The folly was empty. The Firebird might never have existed.

The Eye of Darkness

But as Dominic sought futilely for even the slightest evidence of that fantastic fall to earth, his eyes were drawn to the narrow descending flight of steps, the dark stairway leading down to a concealed bower. Not a fern or a flower had been displaced, and the only possible explanation was that the Firebird had arrowed straight down into the darkness either to shatter itself or—or to lead the way.

Carefully, the boy stood at the top of the steps and peered down. There was no sign of movement or radiance, nothing but a baleful eye of darkness staring back up at him. He stood indecisively for a few moments, trying to estimate the quality of his own courage and the possible reasons for the Firebird's descent—if indeed it had really vanished into the darkness of the bower.

The hesitation did not help. His conviction that the Firebird had gone down into the darkness increased in direct proportion to his own aversion for following it. The black inscrutable eye seemed to become larger, more menacing, until he knew that if he delayed any longer his fear would win.

Consciously blocking his thought and imagination,

Dominic set foot on the first step. Then he ventured further, resolutely telling himself that he was merely going down eight or nine steps into nothing more extraordinary than a small dark room.

The cool air of the grotto rose up to meet him, and he felt as if he were slipping into a pool of night. He refused to count the steps and so they became innumerable, leading perhaps to a cavern at the very centre of the earth.

Eternity passed and there were no more steps. He found himself standing on the floor of the bower. As his eyes became accustomed to the gloom, he saw that what he had imagined as total darkness was nothing more than a sort of deep twilight relieved by a patch of sky which he could still see when looking back up the stairway. A few rays of light also filtered through a small high window which had been set into the wall of the folly just above ground level and which could not be seen at all from the outside, screened as it was by ferns and grasses.

Something was slithering along the floor. Dominic peered anxiously through the gloom and thought that he could make out the shape of a small snake retreating to the far side of the bower. Probably it was a grass snake or a blindworm; but the possibility that it might also be a viper served to justify his apprehension about coming down and restored his self-respect. Viper or not, he was determined to stay until he discovered what had happened to the Firebird, for it was not to be seen.

The wall of the bower, like the outside wall of the folly itself, was circular. Dominic, his mind filled with visions of secret panels and hidden springs, decided to explore every part of it. Surely the Firebird had gone *somewhere*. Such a bright and vital creature could not just cease to be alive.

The slithering of the snake had stopped and, as he moved slowly forward, letting his fingers slide delicately over as much of the smooth stone wall as he could reach, he willed himself not to think about it. So intent was he upon exploring the possibilities of the wall that he did not notice another smaller pool of darkness that opened at his feet.

With the next step that he took, Dominic walked unexpectedly into space. There was a long, terrifying moment of falling—a strange, weightless interval when it seemed as if the whole physical world had suddenly dissolved, leaving him to be carried alone down the river of eternity—then his small body was shaken by a searing impact. Stars exploded in the darkness, cascading in showers of brilliant colours, dazzling and symmetrical as the patterns of a turning kaleidoscope, before they faded into a deep whorl of nothing.

Dominic did not know how far he had fallen or how long he had been unconscious. He was aware only of the ache in his limbs, the rhythmic throbbing in his head, the sense of isolation. Now he was in a world of total darkness, a cold frightening world where the sound of his own voice mocked hollowly as it bounced back at him from hidden walls of silence.

He wanted to die. He wanted the pain and the fear and the loneliness to be swallowed by a state of unbeing. He wanted to live. He wanted daylight and movement, the joy of recognizing himself in a recognizable background. Above all, he wanted to know that what had happened was neither pointless nor cruel, that at least there was a meaning even in disaster.

He was afraid to move, afraid that there might be yet another pit at whose edge he could even now be lying. But as he lay there, waiting and wondering, he was surprised to find that he was becoming curiously calm.

At the same time, shapes seemed to be materializing slowly out of the darkness. He became aware of the uneven contours of the ground ahead and of rough walls that seemed to be part of some kind of tunnel or passage. The air became warmer; and, glancing at his own legs and arms, he saw that they were taking on a subtly golden glow.

As he looked up he saw the source of light. There in the distance, where the passage seemed to open out into a broad cavern, hovered the Firebird.

Dominic scrambled to his feet. The pain and the sense of desolation were forgotten. All that mattered was that he had again found his burning talisman, that he had not yet failed in his pursuit of the creature with the wings of flame.

He gazed in delight at the distant Firebird, drawing strength from its serene radiance, drawing hope and vitality from its dismissal of the unknown dark. He began to run towards the cavern where it was now circling lazily; and as his feet moved over the rough floor of the passage, he suddenly realized that he must now be passing beneath the water of the lake.

He thought idly of the submerged giant he had imagined whose petrified elbow was the island. Perhaps he had fallen down into that gargantuan stomach and was doomed to wander along its dead, endless passages until he became exhausted. No matter! The Firebird was there also, and where the Firebird led he would follow.

A Pin-Point of Light

As Dominic reached the cavern, where the Firebird was now circling high and with gathering speed, he saw that it was like a massive dome whose walls of rock were smooth as a mirror and honeycombed in all directions with small passages and tunnels.

The Firebird was circling at great speed now. It whirled round and round, high and low, executing beautiful curves and parabolas of light, carving bright spirals of fire in the darkness to be mirrored by the walls of the cavern until everywhere was a mobile tracery of flame.

Dominic watched with occasional cries of happiness and wonder. He would not have believed that anything so beautiful could exist—in reality or in dreams. The long swoops, the incredible turns, the swift soarings seemed like a kind of writing on the deep page of space or a sequence of pictures outlined in fire. But after a time it came to Dominic that the Firebird was actually dancing and that it was dancing for him alone.

Suddenly there was one last curved streak across the cavern. Then the Firebird vanished. For a moment or two Dominic was blinded by the darkness;

and until he remembered the innumerable passages he was afraid that the beautiful creature had flown through solid rock where he could not hope to follow. But when his eyes had adjusted to the absence of those brilliant rings and loops of flame, he saw a tiny circular glow on the far side of the dome. That would be the passage the Firebird had entered, and where he was meant to follow.

Carefully he felt his way across the broad rocky floor. The passage from which the glow came was more than the height of his head above the level of the cavern; but there were tiny cracks in the polished wall—deep enough for two fingers here and the tip of a toe there—and inch by inch he was able to haul himself up. The skin was rubbed from his knees and fingers. As he pulled himself up the last few inches into the passage something sharp ripped the soft flesh of his leg, and he felt warm blood trickle slowly down. But he did not mind: he was still able to follow the Firebird.

He could not see it, but the whole passage glowed with its unmistakable light. He ran forward, noticing that the way ahead curved gently and that the ground began to rise. But no matter how fast he ran, he could not catch the Firebird up, though the intensity of its reflected light on the rocky face of the tunnel told him that he could not be far behind. He ran until he could run no more. Then he began to walk; and finally he took to sitting down occasionally for short rests. But always the glow remained constant, fading behind him abruptly into darkness; and always there was the sense of nearness and the consolation that, somehow, the Firebird was aware of his limitations, and that the journey would not be harder than he could bear.

The passage wound steadily upward. Though it

was never steep, the incessant climb made Dominic's legs ache; and presently he began to feel that he had been climbing for ever. His movements became mechanical, then erratic. He began to stumble frequently —not because he did not see the stones in his path but because he could not persuade his exhausted limbs to avoid them. His mind began to play tricks; and in imagination he could see the dance of the Firebird once more—the dizzy spirals, the hypnotic loops, all shrinking into one long awful whirl.

Suddenly he was snatched from his mild delirium by the realization that the fiery glow had disappeared and the passage was now dark. He rubbed his eyes and peered into the darkness. There was nothing— nothing but a pin-point of light directly ahead . . . White light . . . Daylight?

The impact upon him was almost physical. Daylight! It seemed so long now since he had been in the open that he could hardly believe he would once more feel wind and sunlight upon his body.

Dominic gathered his strength and began to walk faster. Despite the darkness in the passage, which had now straightened though it was becoming steeper, he moved with confidence. The Firebird was no longer near to guide him, but perhaps that was only because he would be drawn to the daylight.

The pin-point grew into a circle. The circle widened into a magic window. As he came closer to it, Dominic started to tremble with impatience and anxiety. He saw that the opening was set in the rock much higher than his head. Though it was a wider opening than that of the tunnel leading out of the cavern, with easier purchase for his hands and feet on the uneven rockface, he was afraid he might not have enough strength for the climb.

His fears were unnecessary. The nearness of daylight generated new energy in his body, and he sprang at the rock, scaling it without difficulty.

The energy lasted until he had swung his body up through the gap into an entrancing surface world. Then, before he could even satisfy his curiosity with a glance at his surroundings, fatigue overcame him. He lay there at the edge of the opening, his eyes closed and his heart beating with reproachful thunder.

The Meaning of Heresy

After a time, Dominic recovered himself. He opened his eyes and sat up. He looked around.

At first he had a fleeting impression that he had returned to the folly, having shrunk to a Lilliputian size on the journey; for he was sitting on the floor of a vast semi-circular building whose roof seemed to be lodged in the very sky and was supported by massive, towering columns.

But the difference between this building and the folly was the difference between a house and a cathedral. Apart from its tremendous size, there was an atmosphere of greatness—of greatness and beauty and mystery.

The opening from which Dominic had emerged was perfectly round and set in the middle of a crimson floor that was made of some strange material as smooth and shiny as polished steel, yet warm to the touch. The whole surface seemed to be one single piece and, apart from its warmth, was like a lake of dark frozen blood. On the other side of the hole, set on a tiny pedestal, was a transparent ball of glass or crystal whose diameter was greater than Dominic's outstretched arms. Inside it, imprisoned at the centre, its freshness fixed for all time, was a single red rose. Behind this there was a cone, also of glass or crystal, tapering to a fine point high above the crimson floor, although its base was no greater than the diameter of the ball. Inside the cone, motionless and eternal, was a slender tongue of blue and yellow flame.

There was no further ornament or decoration in the building—nothing but the great columns at the perimeter of the crimson floor: columns of blue-veined marble, so high that it seemed impossible to believe in their reality. The hollow, half-moon roof they supported was glowing brighter than silver and seemed to be dancing in the clouds.

Dominic's excitement bubbled up into exclamations of delight. The building could only be a Temple —the finest that had ever been imagined or created— and the journey he had made would have been worthwhile for the sight of this alone.

But he knew that, wonderful as it was, the Temple was only the beginning. For wherever the Firebird led, there would be beauty and meaning far beyond his ability to understand.

For a while he had lost himself in the sheer glory of his surroundings; but now he was reminded of the creature of flame and radiance that had shown him the way.

Dominic looked all around him. There was no sign of the fiery wings, no bright and sudden sweep through the startled air. He was alone in the great Temple—alone with a sense of pattern and purpose in a world that was as unreal as a dream, or a dream that was more real than the world.

He ran to the edge of the crimson floor and gazed at the surrounding countryside. The Temple stood in a broad valley, the mountains on each side being several miles away—blue and snow-capped. The valley itself curved in a long crescent, so that at first glance it seemed as if the mountains entirely surrounded the Temple as a distant, protective wall. But a broad river rippled along the plain like a grey and green serpent, and Dominic decided that the valley must be a very long one indeed.

The Temple had apparently been built in untamed countryside, for there were no fences or houses anywhere. There were, however, two straight roads, each leading to the foot of the Temple steps. One came up the valley, sometimes bridging the river, sometimes running alongside it, passing through woods and over grassland without any deviation at all. In the same manner, the other came straight down the valley; both of them meeting at the crimson steps.

Nowhere was the Firebird to be seen, and Dominic began to feel depressed. The sun hung in mid-morning splendour over the mountains, its rays giving a warm glow to the strange landscape. But its mood of pleasant optimism was not appreciated by the boy. He was alone in an unknown country.

Yet not quite alone.

Some distance away, on the road leading up the valley, Dominic glimpsed a movement. He could just make out the figure of a man with some kind of small trolley or cart.

Dominic ran down the steps. Down the steps and along the cobblestone road. By the time he came up with the roadmender—for such the man proved to be—he was so much out of breath that he could hardly speak.

The old man, who wore a rough leather tunic and crude sandals, gazed at him curiously.

"Is there such a need to hurry, boy?" he asked with an amused smile. "Life holds a substantial number of days, each day contains no less than twenty-four hours, and each hour is filled with minutes. Do you so bitterly regret the passing of a handful?" There was a lilt in his voice and the words came slow and musically.

"I am a stranger," said Dominic. "I was alone, and I saw you . . . So I came."

"You came indeed," observed the roadmender drily. "You came as one pursued. And now you have arrived and the heavens have not fallen. Sit here and rest."

Dominic sat down on the grass. "You are the first person I have seen this morning," he remarked, feeling the need to say something. He wanted to ask about the Firebird, but held back for a reason he could not understand.

The old man laughed. "And you are the first child I have seen in half a hundred yesterdays. Children do not often visit the Temple of the Firebird." Suddenly he gave Dominic a searching look. "How came you there?"

In his excitement, Dominic ignored the question. "Have you seen it?" he asked anxiously. "I lost it in the darkness and when I came out into the daylight there was nothing at all—except the Temple and—"

"What nonsense is this?" demanded the old man. "What are you talking about, boy?"

"The Firebird," said Dominic patiently. "It must have come out of the Temple. I wondered if you might have seen it . . . You *should* have seen it because—"

"Enough!" The roadmender raised his arm as if to strike. There was anger in his voice. "Many have mocked me on the pilgrimage, for to be a mender of roads is not the highest dignity to which a man may attain, but none have yet mocked the Firebird and lived. Know you the meaning of heresy, boy?" His hand shot out to grab Dominic's shoulder, and strong fingers dug forcefully into his flesh.

Dominic was terrified. "I—I am not mocking the Firebird," he managed to say. "I only wanted to know if you had seen it because I've been following it since dawn and——"

The old man's grip tightened. "That is the heresy!" he roared. "It is written that none shall look upon the Firebird and live. It is written that only in the most divine and holy madness shall even the highest of priests envisage its terrible beauty. It is written that the heretic shall be consumed by its mystic flame . . . What now, child? What do you say now?"

"Please, you're hurting my shoulder," whimpered Dominic. "I'm sorry if I said something wrong. I didn't mean to say anything that would make you angry."

"Penitence will be of little avail when the Four Horsemen ride after you," said the old man grimly. But his grip slackened. "Do you not know that if you continue to speak of seeing the Firebird you will surely be put to the question?"

"Sir, I'm a stranger here," said Dominic, recovering himself a little. "I do not know the ways of this country. But I must follow the Firebird. I must follow it no matter what happens. That is the only thing I know."

"A stranger indeed," remarked the old man, marvelling, "You speak of the Firebird as if such a child as you could be familiar with its terrible presence." Suddenly, he seemed to make up his mind. "See, boy. See this hammer wherewith I break the stones that are to be laid upon the road? Tell your story, and let it be but the truth. For I swear by the invisible presence that if it does not have the ring of truth,

I will crack your skull myself and save the Horsemen a journey. Better a quick death than the eternity of the question."

With surprising agility the old man swung his long hammer through the air and brought it crashing down on a small boulder so that it was completely shattered by the force. "Now speak!"

Dominic swallowed. It seemed to him now that no matter what he said the end would be the same. Either he would tell the truth and be punished for the incomprehensible crime of seeing the Firebird or, if he invented something more acceptable, the roadmender would probably guess that he was lying and carry out his threat.

The boy gave a terrified look at the hammer and the tough, wrinkled hands that gripped its long shaft. Then he made his decision. Better to die for the truth than for what was without meaning.

Brighter Than the Sun

Dominic began to tell his story. He told of his discovery of the ruined cottage and the door that was still standing, and of what happened when he opened the door. As he described his first encounter with the Firebird, he saw the roadmender's hands tighten round the hammer and expected at any moment to see it swing through the air and come crashing down with the deadly gift of darkness. But, miraculously, the hammer did not move; and Dominic went on to tell of his crossing of the lake, the way the Firebird had gone down into the folly and the way he had followed it. He described his journey along the underground passage, the Firebird's dance in the great cavern, and his own eventual emergence in the Temple.

When he had finished there was a taut silence. He did not dare to look at either the old man or his hammer; for he was sure that he had said too much and that the punishment would be swift and final.

But nothing happened.

After a time, the boy dared to meet the road-mender's piercing gaze.

"My son," said the old man, his voice now

strangely gentle, "it seems to me that there are three possible interpretations of this enigma. The first, that what you have said is true—which is manifestly absurd. The second, that you are the most original heretic yet to attempt the corruption of the people of this land—which is also absurd, for a boy could not devise such unusual blasphemy. And the third possibility is that you have been touched by the flame."

"What does that mean?" asked Dominic, more afraid of the roadmender's obvious pity than of his previous anger.

"It means, my son," said the old man softly, "that you are mad."

The boy and the roadmender gazed at each other. Dominic could not bear the look of pity he found in the old man's eyes.

"Sir, I am not mad," he said at last, and with a conviction that surprised him. "I have seen the Firebird."

"Delusions," murmured the roadmender sadly. "Heretical delusions. Speak of them if you must to no one but me, my son, or the Four Horsemen will surely ride . . . Better still, stay with me, share my cottage and help to mend the roads. It is lonely work, and you shall be as my own child . . . If they hunt you I will, at my peril, conceal you. And if it gives you pleasure, my son, I will try to believe in this country from which you say you came—for of a truth your words are strange and your manner is not of the people—but speak no more of seeing the Firebird, I beg. Already I imperil my own salvation."

"I am grateful to you," said Dominic cautiously; and, for a moment, his glance rested on the hammer once more, "but I must go on. I must go on until—" he saw the tough old hands tighten round the shaft—

"until I find the truth for myself," he concluded hastily.

"So be it," answered the roadmender. "Truly, the touch of the flame is upon you."

Dominic looked at the empty roads, stretching on either side of the Temple as far as the eye could see. "Where do the roads lead?" he asked.

The old man laughed. "There are but two great roads in the country of Arcana, and I little thought that I would ever be asked their destinations." He shook his head. "The touch of the flame is surely terrible."

"Where do they go?" persisted Dominic.

"Boy, I will indulge your humour. I will instruct you as if you were properly the stranger you claim to be. From the Temple of the Firebird the two roads lead one to the City and the other to the Forest. In the Forest dwell the People of Darkness; and in the City, the People of Light. The Forest people are peculiar in their habits and it is said that they do not understand even the meaning of heresy. They are sufficiently barbaric to attach more importance to clan loyalty than to the immaculate dogma, whereas the City people are devoted to order and orderly thought. But, despite their differences . . ." The roadmender stopped, having realized that the boy was no longer listening.

There was an expression of intense happiness on Dominic's face. He stood quite still, gazing over the head of the old man. There in the sky the Firebird circled with majestic ease. Even in mid-morning it seemed brighter than the sun, and its blazing aureole seemed to set the whole landscape shimmering.

The roadmender followed Dominic's gaze and saw nothing.

"What is it, boy?" he demanded hoarsely. "There

is a vision in your eyes and glory on your face—such a look belongs only to one who foresees death or miracles. What is it?"

"The Firebird," murmured Dominic, "there over the Temple, making circles of flame."

The roadmender stared fearfully. "I see nothing but the clouds, the blue sky and the morning sun."

"Now it swoops towards the river!"

"Delusion! There is only sunlight on the water."

"And now," went on Dominic, "it is skimming away to the trees."

"Heresy!" roared the old man, trembling, "there is only the wind in the grass." He lifted his hammer slowly and with resolution. "Better for you to die, my son, than be so tormented."

With a sudden joyful bound, Dominic was away. He felt light and powerful and full of purpose again. His feet seemed barely to touch the ground. "Goodbye!" he called. "I must follow where the Firebird leads!"

Too late the old man's hammer thundered down on the spot where he had stood.

The roadmender watched the boy, who had left the road and was running across rough grassland, leaping impatiently over small shrubs and bushes in his path. The roadmender rubbed his eyes. Was it a trick of light or the imagination—or was this boy, whose tongue confessed madness and whose eyes saw that which could not be, was he really gaining in strength and stature as he moved?

The old man watched until Dominic was out of sight. Then he rubbed his eyes once more and shook his head. "Of a truth," he said, "the touch of the flame troubles him most grievously, and the Four Horsemen will surely ride, since his heresy endangers the people."

With a sigh, the old man lifted his long hammer and resumed the breaking of stones. Up went his arms, then down came the hammer. Up and down, up and down—the rhythm became fast and fierce, as if the roadmender had sought heresy in the very stones he used and was determined to pave the way to the Temple only with the purest fragments.

A Sense of Belonging

Meanwhile, Dominic pursued the Firebird.

It seemed at times that the creature of radiance was bound to him by an invisible cord, that the cord pulled him along, lifting him over obstacles, relentlessly drawing him along the path he must take. His body felt oddly revitalized, his stride seemed longer, his spirit more confident. Yet, at the same time he was aware of a curious element of detachment. Even as he followed the Firebird he was able to stand apart, as it were, and observe the chase with the calm appreciation of a spectator.

Already, the events of the early morning seemed to have happened a long time ago—so long ago, indeed, that the small boy who had slipped through the doorway of a ruined cottage in the solitude of dawn seemed almost to be another person. Only a few hours had passed, for the sun had not yet reached the height of noon, yet Dominic now felt as if his crossing of the lake and his subterranean journey had taken years to accomplish or had happened in another kind of time.

So preoccupied did he become with his odd confusion over the passage of time that he was not actually aware of the exact moment of losing the Firebird. His pursuit had developed into an almost unconscious response; and it was only when he was aware of a sudden loss of direction, a slackening of the invisible cord, a shadow passing in some dimension not of space or time, that he realized the Firebird had vanished.

He was in a pleasant glade now, surrounded by tall and mature trees. Even as he realized that the Firebird had disappeared once more, his legs stopped moving, as if the source of energy had suddenly been withdrawn; and he stood there, bewildered.

The clearing was small. The leaves and branches of great trees on every side intermingled high above the ground, forming a green roof that seemed to glow softly under the oblique sunlight and through which hundreds of tiny irregular patches of pale blue sky looked like part of a distant stretch of calm water.

The grass beneath Dominic's feet was short and soft and luminous, challenging even the brightness of the leaves. He thought that here would be a good place to rest quietly, to consider his situation—and, perhaps, wait until the Firebird returned. For he was sure it would return.

There was, he decided as he lay down and stretched luxuriously upon the grass, a mutual dependence. In some way and for some reason that he could not understand, he and the Firebird belonged to each other, needed each other. For he knew now that he was only properly alive when he was in pursuit of it—just as it, perhaps, could only generate its beautiful radiance for eyes that were capable of seeing.

Dominic gazed drowsily up through the roof of green and thought about this aspect of the relationship. He was surprised by the nature of his own thoughts—surprised even that he could consider the Firebird so dispassionately. Perhaps he was learning to grow up—or simply learning . . .

After a time, his thoughts turned to the road-mender and what he had been told about the country in which he now found himself. Arcana was its name, he remembered, and it seemed to be a very strange land with its People of Light and People of Darkness, and the two great roads.

It was a land, he felt, where he would always remain a stranger. No matter how long he stayed he would always feel apart because he saw what it was forbidden to see and because he followed what it was forbidden to follow. Perhaps, as the roadmender had said, he was mad. Or perhaps he was simply one who could see among those who were blind.

The thought of the solitude—and the danger—he might have to endure frightened him; and he began to wonder whether it might not be more comfortable, even more satisfying, to be blind. But then an image of the Firebird drifted into his mind, and the memory of its radiance was enough to convince him that life without such vision would be very dull indeed. There would be nothing to do but live, grow old and then die. Whereas the pursuit of the Firebird offered at the very least a reason for being alive. It gave purpose to a random journey. It created strange and indescribable patterns of feeling in his heart; a sense of belonging, moments of ecstasy and glimpses of perfection that were enough to justify whatever privation or danger the world would impose . . .

Lying there on the grass was pleasant. After a time Dominic grew tired of staring up at the green leaves and the tiny patches of sky. He closed his eyes and let him mind wander lazily down warm avenues of darkness. Presently he was asleep.

The Girl With Green Hair

The next thing of which Dominic was aware was a small cool hand moving lightly over his face. Restraining an impulse to move, he kept his eyes closed and tried to determine entirely by the touch what kind of person was exploring his features with such care. Obviously it was not a man. The fingers were soft and sensitive. They must belong either to a child or a woman.

However, the voice he then heard seemed to belong neither to a child nor a woman but to someone who was, perhaps, a little of both.

"Waken up!" she commanded impatiently. "Waken up, I say! Would you sleep your whole life through?"

Dominic opened his eyes and sat up. The girl beside him was lithe and slender. Her arms and legs and face were a golden brown. She was barefoot and her only clothing appeared to be a kind of short green gown. Her eyes were large and green and full of mischief. But what startled Dominic was the long lustrous hair hanging carelessly about her shoulders.

"Your hair is green!" he exclaimed.

"So are my eyes," she said unconcernedly. "They match perfectly. What is so peculiar about that?"

"I've never seen anyone with hair the colour of grass."

"And I have never seen anyone with hair the colour of ripe corn," she remarked. "Furthermore, your eyes are blue and they do not match your hair at all, which is exceedingly curious."

"I didn't mean to be rude," apologized Dominic, "but in my country no one has green hair."

She regarded him with amusement. "In my country," she mimicked, "it is fashionable to have hair and eyes of the same colour. You are certainly an odd person and quite possibly touched by the flame. You may kiss me."

Dominic stood up and made an embarrassed gesture towards her cheek. She appeared to be enjoying herself hugely.

"No, on the lips," she said regally. "Are you *so* uncivilized?"

He meant to touch her lightly; but she clung hard against him for a second or two and her lips were strangely sweet. Then she sprang away, laughing.

He gazed at her uncertainly, not knowing what was expected of him. He had a sudden, tempting urge to run away, but he would rather have died than give in to it.

"My name is Dominic," he managed at last.

"I do not need a name," she flashed, her eyes glittering. "My mother was a forest and my father was a storm cloud. I was conceived where the lightning struck."

Dominic's feeling of bewilderment increased. In desperation he tried to think of some intelligent comment to make, but there didn't seem to be any. Finally, he decided to tell her about his journey.

"I am looking for the Firebird," he said. "Can you help me?"

Her eyes widened. "You have certainly been touched by the flame. No one looks for that which can never be seen. Besides, it is what they call heresy, which is quite a serious condition, I believe . . . Now *I* am looking for a youth whose mother was a snow-capped mountain and whose father was the burning sun. Can *you* help *me?*"

"No . . . At least, I don't think so."

She tossed her green hair. "You would be sure if you were the one, and you would be sure if you were not. On the other hand, it is possible you are so disguised that you cannot even recognize yourself. Perhaps I will help you to find out."

Suddenly, she sprang at him with such force that they both fell to the grass, rolling down into a small hollow. When they came to rest, Dominic found that his arms were round the girl with green hair, and that her hard and slender body seemed to have turned surprisingly soft.

"Kiss me," she whispered. "I want to know. You need to know."

This time her lips were softer and more sweet with mystery. He was surprised at the pleasure growing within him, disturbed at the urgency. He felt as if he had discovered something so fragile that a single touch would destroy it. He felt as if he had discovered the elusive secret of life and would have to hold tight to prevent its escape.

Dominic kissed her again, and the feeling of confusion increased.

"You are too gentle," she murmured. "*He* would hold me in the grip of ice and sear me with a dark flame . . . No, boy with the hair like corn, you are not the one. Or perhaps your disguise is still too heavy to penetrate."

She broke away quickly and sat back on her heels,

gazing down at Dominic's serious face with laughter in her eyes.

He was afraid of her mockery, and the fear turned to anger. "You are the one who has been touched by the flame," he cried. "You call yourself a child of the storm and the forest—why, you are nothing but a green-haired girl with green eyes and green dreams in a green heart. Who would want a girl of only one colour? You will not outlast the summer. By autumn you will be dry and lifeless. And when winter comes you will have returned to the earth; and there will be nothing left to remember but a colour. Nothing but the memory of green."

He was so angry that the words tumbled out and he did not understand them. He did not even know if there was any meaning in them at all. But their effect on the girl was startling.

The laughter went from her eyes and was replaced by such a look of misery that Dominic was appalled by what he immediately regarded as his own unprovoked cruelty. Tears rolled down her cheeks, and her body began to shake with an uncontrollable sobbing.

"It's not true," she moaned. "Please say it's not true. I want to be green for ever in a green world."

He put his arms round her, stroking the long green hair and trying to comfort her. "I was lying," he said gently. "You shall be green for ever."

"No," she whispered. "It is now that you are lying. There is such a look on your face—the look of one who sees." Then she glanced up at him and smiled. "No matter. I shall not think about the things I do not want to understand. I shall not even think about tomorrow. I am alive, and that is enough."

Suddenly she jumped to her feet. "There is a stream not far from here where brown-backed fish hide in the shadow of stones and water weed. I will show you how to catch them, and we will kindle a fire and eat their white flesh. I will show you where to find the early berries and how to drink clear water from a green-leaf goblet, and we will steal eggs from the wild birds . . . Come."

The Four Horsemen

The green-haired girl took him by the hand. Presently they reached the bank of a wide but shallow stream flowing lazily to join the deep waters of the river that Dominic had seen from the Temple. She showed him how to stand motionless by large stones and scoop the fish, flashing in sunlight, out on to the bank, where their silver bellies gleamed and quivered as they died. She showed him how to make fire with nothing but dry twigs and brittle leaves.

Presently a thin spiral of smoke rose by the bank of the stream, and the fish began to spit and sizzle in the heat of the growing flames.

Dominic thought that they had taken more from the stream than they could eat; but he had not realized how hungry he was or how sweet was the taste of food. They washed the fish down with long draughts of water. Then, while Dominic lay down and basked in the sunlight, the green-haired girl disappeared for a while to return with a handful of berries and a few pale blue eggs.

"Stay with me," she said abruptly when they could eat no more. "Stay and share with me the wind and the rain, the sunlight and the sounds of life."

Dominic sighed. "I do not think I was meant to stay anywhere."

She pouted. "Why must you be so restless? It is against nature always to be a wanderer. There is a time to move and a time to stay."

Dominic stretched lazily and gazed at the stream flowing almost at his feet. "I am like the stream," he said. "I must always go on."

"The stream is drawn to the river," she retorted slyly, "and then it is no longer a stream. It is lost in something greater."

He smiled. "And I am drawn to the Firebird. Perhaps if I should ever touch it I, too, should be lost in something greater."

The girl moved closer to him; and as they lay side by side on the grass, her hand came to rest upon his arm.

"I will tell you what I would tell no other," she murmured. "I, too, am a heretic."

Dominic gazed at her, startled.

"You say you have seen the Firebird," she went on, "and *they* say it cannot be seen." She smiled impishly. "Personally, I do not believe that there is any such thing—visible or invisible."

But Dominic was hardly aware of her words, for there was a feeling of thunder in the ground. The earth seemed to tremble, and the vibrations were echoed through his body.

"Horsemen," said the girl unconcernedly. "Possibly the Four . . . They are coming this way. Perhaps they have seen the smoke above the trees."

Dominic was afraid. "The Four Horsemen! Why should they come here?"

"To seek heretics—why else? That is their purpose."

The rhythm of the hoofs slowed down, but it was stronger, more insistent.

"Perhaps," added the girl calmly, "they are looking for you."

"Or for both of us," said Dominic with emphasis. "Where can we hide?"

"We cannot both hide, for they will see the fire and then they will seek us. You will hide and I will stay."

"But—"

"Away!" cried the girl impatiently. "Your heresy is necessary to you. It is in your face and in your eyes. Mine does not matter to me. It sits but loosely in my mind. I will believe what they wish me to believe. I am too silly to be a true heretic, too simple to be put to the question . . . Hurry! I see the sunlight on their masks."

"Where must I go?"

She laughed. "Horsemen do not ride the tree-tops. But hide your head, boy with hair like ripe corn, for no tree bears such golden fruit."

Dominic found a tall pine tree whose branches swung out stiffly from the trunk, providing firm if irregular footholds that climbed in an ever narrowing spiral. Up and up he went, while the tree seemed to be growing ever taller. At last he came to a point where the trunk was too slender for him to go on. So he sat astride the last firm branch and made himself comfortable. Then he looked down.

There had been no time to spare. As he peered through the intricate screen of branches and pine needles, he saw that the Four Horsemen had already reached the stream and were advancing in a leisurely way towards the girl with green hair.

Each rider was clothed from head to foot in mail, and each wore a silver mask, smooth and contourless, covering the whole face except for narrow eye-slits. One carried a drawn sword and one a slender lance. The remaining two were armed with mace and battleaxe. But, apart from the difference of weapons, all four were indistinguishable.

"In the name of the Inquisitors," said the Sword, "Greetings!" His voice was loud and carried easily through the still air to the top of the pine tree.

"In the name of the Question," answered the girl, "Greetings." Dominic marvelled at the confidence in her voice and the innocence with which she regarded the Four Horsemen.

"There is heresy abroad," said the Lance. "Therefore we seek it."

"If there is heresy," she answered in tones of evident fear, "the Four Horsemen will surely find it."

"Girl," said the Mace, "one who has passed this way is touched by the flame. He mocks that which may not be mocked: he sees that which may not be seen. Know you of such a one?"

The terror in the voice of the girl seemed to Dominic, as he sat motionless in the tree-top, to be completely genuine. "I have seen only a boy," she said, "a boy with golden hair and blue eyes and a strange manner of speech . . . There did not seem to be any great madness in him. I spoke with him and gave him fish to eat." She sank to her knees. "Have I then sinned?"

"In ignorance," said the Axe, towering above her, "you have sinned, but the sin is not mortal. Where now is the golden one, child?"

"He spoke with excitement of what I did not understand," she answered timidly. "Then he crossed the stream and passed through the woods with great speed . . . Is he doomed?"

"He is doomed," said the Sword.

"Pray for him," commanded the Lance.

"He will have need of prayer," added the Mace grimly.

"Forward!" shouted the Axe.

The Four Horsemen rode at the stream, each clearing it in a mighty leap. Presently they were lost to view among the trees; and after a time, the thunder of hooves died into silence.

Dominic came down from the pine tree.

"Strength to the Four Horsemen!" cried the girl gaily. "They will ride hard this day. They will ride the length and breadth of Arcana."

"Aren't you afraid they will return?"

"Sir," she said with irony, "I am but a poor green-haired girl and know nothing of the ways of the great ones . . . And if they return, what then? By that time the falsehood will have become truth, for I see in your eyes that you will never stay."

"You do indeed see the truth," said Dominic in a strange, far away voice.

For there over the stream hovered the Firebird— poised like a great burning kingfisher for the strike. In the shimmering radiance even the stream itself had become as a rivulet of fire; and the noon stillness quivered like music through a million dancing leaves. And power shone from the Firebird in dazzling waves of light.

The invisible cord pulled at Dominic, and the power surged through his limbs.

"What is it?" asked the girl with sudden fear. "You have the look of one who must endure greatness or madness. What do you see now?"

"The Firebird," he answered softly, "there over the stream."

"Is it not a shaft of sunlight arrowing between the trees?"

"It is the Firebird."

"Or a trick of the light upon water?" she added desperately.

"It is the Firebird."

Almost lazily, the creature of flame swung to the far side of the stream, gliding towards the trees on outstretched burning wings.

"Goodbye, girl with green hair. I follow where you cannot."

"Goodbye, boy whose heart has been touched by the flame," she called. "Remember me!"

Then Dominic was across the stream in pursuit of the Firebird with the long strides of one who might yet attain the stature of a man among men.

Sunlight Upon Silver

The brilliant, fiery wings were now beating the air rhythmically. The Firebird began to move quickly, and so did Dominic. The feeling of power was rippling through his limbs like music; the tide sang in his veins, and he was drunk with invincibility. There was nothing he could not do—no mountain he could not climb, no enemy he could not vanquish. So long as the Firebird led the way, so long as he was held to it by the invisible cord.

Through the woods and out into the open country he ran, across heath and grassland and marsh, over hummocks and gullies, across streams and even along the great road that led from the Temple to the Forest. The Firebird was dancing for him. It danced high and low, etching the journey in transient patterns of flame. And through the long golden afternoon, Dominic ran, not knowing or caring if the pursuit should last for ever.

In the distance there was the Forest, stretching dark and heavy across the land—rank upon rank of trees of tremendous height. As he came closer, he saw that their trunks were like rough-carved pillars set deep into the earth. Their leaves were heavy, sombre, presenting the sunlight with an impenetrable barrier. The Forest was a world of its own.

On and on towards it the Firebird danced, its bright shape gathering an even more intense lustre against the darkness of the now towering line of trees stretching far away on either side. And there at the edge of the Forest, the creature of flame rose suddenly. High into the air it winged until it became small as a daytime star. The star glittered for a moment, then disappeared into the high blue haze of mid-afternoon.

Dominic was alone.

He stared wonderingly at the Forest. It was not at all like the sprawling patch of woodland where he had encountered the girl with green hair. The Forest was darkly primeval, a place of fear and visions and unseen eyes. A place of mystery and danger where none but the desperate would venture.

Dominic was tempted to turn away. But then he remembered that he had been led to the Forest by the Firebird. There must be a purpose in the journey, or if no purpose at least a pattern whose shape would have meaning. It was unthinkable that the long, intricate pursuit should be no more than a game of hide and seek on the grand scale. It was unthinkable because the Firebird itself was a strange and beautiful mystery. It had shown Dominic the way to a land of mysteries and was guiding him, he felt sure, to the very source of life.

Besides, he knew that he would only find it once more—if at all—in the Forest. Therefore into the Forest he must go.

Before he passed the forbidding frontier of trees he looked back over the sun drenched country through which he has passed. This country of Arcana was indeed a beautiful land, he thought. In such a land one might happily spend the rest of one's days; living close to the earth and taking pleasure in the change of the seasons; inspiring the growth of love, perhaps, in one such as the green-haired girl; and, in the course of time, generating the brief and happy immortality of children . . . But for this unending pursuit of the Firebird and the strange crime of heresy it evidently inspired.

Why, thought Dominic, should it be considered wrong to see what was so beautiful, so pure, so full of power and significance? What harm could his pursuit of such a creature do to others? Perhaps they only used heresy as a way of describing whatever they themselves could not hope to see, whatever was strange and beautiful, greater than the power of men and beyond their understanding.

Suddenly he noticed a cloud of dust far away in the broad valley. There was the flash of sunlight upon silver and, in the ground at his feet, a faint but ominous throbbing.

The Four Horsemen! Already they were following him once more. Dominic turned quickly and stepped into the Forest.

The darkness closed round him like a shroud. He stumbled on; and after a time his eyes became accustomed to the gloom. Now and then he heard rustlings and footsteps, sometimes ahead of him, sometimes behind, and sometimes on each side. It was strange, he thought, that he was not greatly afraid. But he felt taller, more confident, and there was power in his limbs and endurance in his heart —far greater now than the power and endurance of a child at dawn.

"Stay, my son! We have met each other and the meeting was foretold. I have waited for you. Come!"

An old man had stepped in Dominic's path. In the half-darkness he seemed more like a phantom than a living person. He was dressed in a long, shapeless, tattered robe. His face was grey and wrinkled. Wisps of beard hung from his chin, and when he smiled Dominic could see the black and broken teeth in his mouth.

"Come, my son! You bring the secret for which I have waited all the days of my life." He stepped closer, and his breath was foul.

"Who are you?"

The old man laughed. "I am your father, your spiritual brother, your true and only child. Come!"

He turned to lead the way. Dominic, filled with curiosity, decided to follow. The old man was loathsome and fascinating. There was an air of knowledge and power about him—and an air of death.

A Fountain of Sparks

He walked with the old man in silence, but the silence did not last long for Dominic became aware of the sound of birds. It was like the crying and wailing of thousands of children, far, far away. He had never heard such a weird sound before. It was full of such despair, such bitter unhappiness, that his own spirit sank also; but the old man appeared to be quite unmoved by the tragic chorus and led the way with a firm step.

The sound grew. Presently they came to a patch of ground that had been cleared of undergrowth and shrubs—a stretch of earth that was without a single blade of grass.

An astounding sight met Dominic's eyes.

In the middle of the barren stretch of ground was a pit; and from the pit thick dull flames leapt and cavorted, giving an orange glow to the scorched earth. By the side of the pit there was a small pile of bars of dull grey metal, and across the pile there lay a length of fine golden chain. But the most fantastic aspect of the scene was the far side of the pit where rows of cages, each containing a bird, were arranged in a great semi-circular wall, one row on top of another, so that their occupants faced the flames.

There were swallows, doves, thrushes, nightingales, sparrows, blackbirds, crows, larks, robins, cuckoos and magpies. There were owls, falcons, eagles, storks, kingfishers, gulls, kites, pheasant, partridges, woodpeckers and starlings. There was every kind of wild bird a prisoner of terror by the burning pit. Piteous and hopeless cries rose from all their cages to be swallowed in the grim darkness of the Forest.

The old man turned and smiled his empty smile. "Here are all my family," he said, "and you shall tell me which is the one. I have tested thousands, but never the right one. You shall tell me which it is, for you will know. You have seen it."

"Old man, you talk in riddles," said Dominic unable to take his eyes from the terrible wall of cages. "But enough of that. First I will set your prisoners free, and then——" he glanced grimly at the malevolent face of his companion, and moved towards the cages.

"I speak of the Firebird," said the old man. "I speak of that which may not be spoken and that which may not be seen. But *you* have seen. It is in your eyes. Therefore you will know the one."

"Old man, you are mad."

There was a dry, harsh laugh. "Well said! We are both touched by the flame, you and I. But listen, I will tell you why the Firebird may not be seen by those who lack the gift of vision. It is because this creature of radiance and power, the winged elixir, the living lode-star, can assume the shape of an ordinary wild bird . . . That is why I lay my traps throughout the Forest, that is why I spend my days putting these miserable creatures to the test. For one day—one day I shall find a bird that will endure.

And that will be the Firebird, whose lightest touch will surely transmute lead into gold."

Dominic gazed at the old man to whose grey face the orange flames brought an eerie glow. He felt a cold anger growing inside him, harder than ice, sharp and violent and deadly.

"Old man," he said in a voice that was ominously gentle, "what is the test to which you put these poor birds? Tell me, for I have truly seen the Firebird, and it is necessary to my judgement."

The old man grinned. "Now that you have come, my son, my brother, the test will no longer be needed. You will look and you will know. The Firebird cannot maintain its disguise for one who has once seen it."

"Nevertheless, tell me."

"Surely, my son, my brother." He laughed once more. "There can be no secrets between your heart and mine . . . The Firebird was born of fire and by fire it cannot be consumed. Therefore I take my wild ones, fasten their legs to the golden chain which you see lying by my store of lead, and cast them alive into the flames. Till now there are none that have risen, none that have defied the flames, none whose touch has turned the lead to gold, making me the master of the world . . . But now you have come, my son, and the search will soon be ended."

"For you," said Dominic, walking round the pit of fire to the cages, "the search is already ended." He broke the fastening on the first cage and set its occupant—a nightingale—free.

The small bewildered bird flew crazily in circles for a moment or two then, finding its movement was not an illusion, soared joyously up through the darkness of the Forest, up towards the blessed daylight.

Dominic dealt with the next cage, and then another and the one after that. A blackbird, a starling and a robin followed the nightingale. The rest of the birds set up such a crying and calling that it was as if they realized liberation was near.

"What are you doing?" screeched the old man angrily. "You are not looking at them. You are not looking for the one!"

"Nor shall I," retorted Dominic, letting loose a pheasant and a dove. "The Firebird cannot be found in a cage, madman. As you took their freedom, so I return it. Let that be enough."

"Fool, you would destroy my life's work!" roared the old man. He seized one of the bars of lead from the pile and rushed at Dominic. "I will kill you. The Firebird shall be mine!"

Dominic whirled and stepped nimbly aside so that the lead bar, instead of shattering his skull, merely grazed his shoulder. Pain dimmed his vision for a moment; but he caught the old man's arm and gripped it so tightly that the heavy bar fell from his fingers.

Dominic seemed to tower above the one who had tried to kill him. He looked down at a face twisted with hate and fury—an evil face void of humanity, beyond redemption.

"Old man," said Dominic softly, "you have outlived your right to live. Seek the Firebird, then, in your own way and with your own body!"

With a sudden movement, he picked the obscene struggling creature up and hurled him bodily into the pit of fire. There was a short, high-pitched scream and a fountain of sparks. The fire crackled and orange flames leapt high for a moment, then settled down to burn softly and fully as before.

Dominic stared at the fire, hardly realizing what

he had done, then he returned to his attack upon the fastenings of the cages. He worked quickly and methodically. Bird after bird soared freely and joyously up through the Forest gloom to the remote blue sky.

It was hard to believe there were so many. Dominic's hands ached with snapping the small wooden fastenings and opening cage doors. But presently there were only three birds still imprisoned. As he paused and surveyed the litter of broken cages with satisfaction, he became aware of what he had been too busy to notice while he worked.

There was a faint throbbing in the ground, a subdued and recognizable thunder. The Four Horsemen must have already entered the Forest.

Hurriedly Dominic released the three remaining birds.

The leisurely rhythm of hooves was perceptibly stronger.

Most of all, he wanted to get away from this place of terror and death, this scene of insane futility. He wanted to put the memory of the old man and all the tormented birds behind him.

It was hard to determine from which direction the Horsemen were riding; but Dominic listened carefully. After a time he decided that they must be following the path along which the old man had led him. So he set off in the opposite direction, plunging deeper into the Forest.

A Time of Death and Resurrection

As Dominic ran he was aware of fatigue and looked hopefully about him for a sign of the Firebird. But there was no exhilerating radiance, no tug of the invisible cord, no mysterious resurgence of vitality. On and on he stumbled, while the thorns and bushes tore at him and all the sharp stones in the world seemed to have been placed in his path.

He had no way of knowing how long he wandered in the Forest twilight. It seemed at times that he had always been surrounded by the high, impassive trees; that the Forest itself was the entire world and he the only human being left alive.

He was filled with an intense loneliness. Such a loneliness, he felt, had never been experienced by anyone before. It was absolute. It drifted, an invisible ghost, throughout the endless gloom and entered his body with every breath he took. It dripped from the high tree-tops, oozed from the moist ground, and hung all about him like a tattered cloak of desolation.

Just as there was no end to it, so there could never have been a beginning. This, thought Dominic hopelessly as he wandered among trees that seemed exactly the same as those he had passed a long time ago, was the whole of life— total loneliness, a solitary journey from nowhere to nowhere. An exploration without hope.

But, suddenly, he found himself at the edge of a large island in the Forest. An island of sky and sunlight. An island of sweet green grass and wild flowers and a feeling of peace.

There was a small tumbledown house standing by the bank of a lake that was hardly more than a broad pool. As he came nearer, Dominic heard a splashing and saw smooth rings of ripples spreading over the surface of the water. There was a woman bathing. As Dominic made his way round the pool towards the cottage, they saw each other at the same time.

"Greetings," called the woman, swimming lazily near the bank. "So you have come at last." Sunlight through the clear water had transformed her body into that of a slender white fish.

"I am a stranger," said Dominic, thinking that she must have mistaken him for someone else.

The woman laughed, and brushed the hair back over her forehead so that it trailed behind her in the water like strands of fine black weed. "All men are strangers . . . Come, now, and wash the day's dust from your body while the sun is still warm enough to dry it afterwards."

Dominic looked at her and at the cool water. Then he began to tear off his clothes. In a few moments he, too, was naked; and the feeling of freedom was intoxicating.

Cautiously, he put a foot into the water. The sudden coolness sent a shiver of delight through his body.

Swimming close, the woman splashed him playfully. Then he plunged in after her, and she led him halfway round the lake, diving suddenly when he came near enough to touch her, and swimming with such ease and speed along the sandy bed that it seemed at times as if the water was her true home.

Try as he might, Dominic could not catch her. But, after a while, she turned and came towards him, taking his hand.

"Let us dry ourselves now," she said. "And you shall tell me whence you have come, for I see that there is a light in your eyes and also a darkness that I do not understand."

Together they returned to the bank in front of the tumbledown house. The woman walked unconcernedly out of the water and lay down on the grass, motioning Dominic to sit by her side. The sunlight seemed to lie intimately across both their bodies like a warm blanket of tranquility that would never be disturbed.

Dominic saw that she was truly beautiful—and at the same time conscious and unconscious of her own shapely body. She had spread her long black hair out to dry, like a fan upon the grass. As he gazed at her, Dominic had the brief illusion that the shiny wet tresses were delicate roots anchoring her firmly to the earth.

Her eyes were also dark—dark and luminous, and full of the wisdom of centuries. Yet she was neither old nor young, simply a woman of great beauty whose full breasts and rounded hips and delicately sturdy legs promised fertility and fulfillment—the strange richness of love.

"I have always known you would come," she said softly, "and I was afraid." She smiled. "But when I saw you the fear died and was replaced by a different one. But there will be time enough to talk of such things when the time comes . . . Did you know that you were looking for me?"

He shook his head. "I was looking for the Firebird. I have been following it for a long time—so long that I can hardly remember what it was like before . . ." He hesitated.

"Before you opened the door."

Dominic was startled. "How do you know about the door?"

She sighed. "There is always a door—one, perhaps, that should not be opened. Many try the handle, then turn away with relief. But there is always someone who must enter—and you are such a one . . . . It is not the only door you have opened. That is why I am both happy and afraid."

"You are a strange woman. You seem to know so much, and yet—"

"And yet," she laughed, "there is so much that I shall never know, so much that is clouded in your eyes . . . Do you like me?"

"Yes." Dominic felt the need to introduce himself. "My name is—"

She placed a finger on his lips. "No names," she said softly. "You are man and I am woman. It is enough . . . Do you think that you could love me?"

He looked at her in bewilderment. "You are very beautiful."

She took his hand and placed it upon her breast. "Then you will love me for a little while because you think I am beautiful."

Dominic's hand seemed to have a will of its own and cupped the breast tightly so that he could feel the sudden secret tremors, the pulse of excitement surging irresistibly through her body. His heart was racing. There was fire in his limbs. The sense of touch, the message of eyes and the incredible nearness all commanded him.

"No one else will ever be so beautiful," he managed to say.

"And you will swear by what you hold, which none shall hold hereafter, that you will remember our love?"

"I swear it." His arm slipped under her head and round her shoulders, disturbing the shiny black fan of hair.

She shivered slightly. "Let the memory always be bright," she murmured. "Bright as the sky above and burning like the sun, and cool and clear like the quiet water." She closed her eyes and lay quietly in his arms, letting her body become impersonal in its loveliness.

For Dominic there was a conflict between the fierceness of desire and a terrifying gentleness. He wanted to crush her, to make her cry out with pain and ecstasy and fear and frenzy. He wanted to hold her like that for ever, holding her only with his eyes so that no effort or compulsion or harshness would ever break the fragile moment of submission.

He looked at her; and the necessity came like a storm, raging through his hands and arms and body, whipped to a hurricane of impatience even in the lonely citadel of his head.

His arms tightened with all the cruelty of love. His body held hers close to the earth as if, otherwise, its lightness might cause it to drift away and be lost to his touch. As he let the urgency of his limbs lie heavily upon her, crushing her breasts against his, and thrusting himself into the warm and secret sheath of her flesh as if he would reach the source of life, a small cry escaped her. It seemed to come not from her throat, but from the depths of her being—a cry of acceptance and despair. A defeated cry of victory.

The movement became a rhythm; the rhythm became a hypnotic dance; the dance became a ritual of annihilation. And the ritual exploded into climax as life became joined to life, seeking to generate life, in the long throbbing moments of release.

For Dominic there was a time of darkness and tranquility. A time of death and resurrection.

Stronger Than Love

Afterwards, he lay quietly with his head on her breast, delighting in the intimate scent of her body. And the world was curiously still.

Presently she spoke. "Pray that I have conceived, my love—for of our embrace a true love-child only could be born. And I will pray that he shall be straight-limbed and with golden hair, growing into a man such as the man who held me. Then there will be a living image to keep the memory of this day bright."

Dominic raised himself and gazed at her. There was fulfilment in her eyes. Fulfilment and sadness.

"I wish that I could stay," he said gently.

"But you will go."

"I wish that I could forget, that I could belong to you now and always."

She smiled. "But you will go. You opened a door and you came. Now you have opened another door and you will go away . . . I have heard of the Fire-bird, though you are the only one I have known who has seen it. I do not understand the nature of your journey, my dear one, except that I know it is one that must be made. But before you go I would have you tell me whence you came, where you have journeyed, what you have seen and hoped . . . Then one day your story shall be told again, for surely I have conceived."

Dominic touched her forehead lightly with his lips. "There is so little to tell," he said. I came from a world of darkness into a world of dawn. I opened a door and saw a vision. And my spirit seemed to know that this vision was the only true reality. So I followed wherever it led—even through a world of dreams."

"I want to know about the journey," she insisted. "I want to know all that has happened. I want to try to understand."

Dominic lay back and gazed silently for a moment or two at the deepening blue of the sky. Then he began to speak. He told her of the great house in which he had been born; of his family who now seemed remote and shadowy; and of the ruined cottage where he had discovered the door. He told her how the Firebird had led him across the lake and how it had seemed to disappear in the earth. He told her of the long, dark passage; of the brilliant, fiery dance in the dome-like cavern; and of his own eventual return to daylight in the Temple. He told her of the roadmender and the girl with green hair, and how he had found and destroyed the old man who imprisoned birds.

When he had finished she, too, lay silent for a while, her hand resting so lightly on his arm that he was almost unaware of its touch.

"I am glad the old man is dead," she said at last. "I am glad that you were the cause of his destruction. Now the Forest will be clean once more, and I shall no longer be afraid."

"You knew him?" asked Dominic. He saw that she was trembling.

"I knew him." Her voice seemed strangely distant. "He was my father."

"I—I am sorry." Dominic was appalled.

Suddenly she roused herself and sat up, looking at him with eyes filled with tenderness. "Do not be sorry, my dearest love. You have taken away the threat of darkness and now I am truly myself. You have broken a nightmare and given me freedom. Do not be sorry, my own true heart; for life shall be renewed by life, and surely your seed lies in my womb." She smiled. "I shall bear a son who is strong and golden, a son who is hard and gentle and so much alive that the earth and the sky will rejoice in his manhood. . . This and the freedom of the birds shall be our atonement."

"But he was your father!" Dominic found it hard to believe that such a foul and despicable creature could have been connected in any way at all with the woman by his side.

"My mother," she answered bitterly, "was no more to him than one of the wild birds he had caught. She lived and died a prisoner of fear. All she could ever give me was her love and her fear. Now you have destroyed the fear and only love remains."

He held her hand, and they gazed at each other for a while without speaking.

Presently she let her head rest upon his shoulder. "It is said that none may see the Firebird and live, yet you have seen it."

He began to stroke her hair. "Yes, I have seen it."

"Tell me what it is like." She sighed. "I should not ask. It should be enough for me to know that the Firebird is stronger than love—strong enough to draw you to follow it for ever . . . And yet . . ." She sighed once more.

"It is brigther than the sun," he said gently. "It

is a vision of purity and purpose, a dream of perfection, a feeling of peace and power and violence and truth. It is a fiery writing in the sky, a lantern in the darkness, a radiance of absolute beauty. To see it once is to see the living mystery of all things." He shook his head sadly. "No, I cannot describe the Firebird. It is simply the light I must follow."

As he spoke he became aware of a curious tension in his limbs. The earth seemed to be quivering faintly; and then the quivering became a rhythmic throb. He and the woman looked at each other anxiously, listening. Within a few moments the throbbing had grown into audible hoofbeats.

"The Four Horsemen!" exclaimed Dominic in dismay. He had been so lost in the enchantment of finding the woman, of discovering her love, that for a while he had almost forgotten the inexorable pursuit.

She jumped to her feet and gazed apprehensively across the small pool at the dark ring of trees.

"Quick!" she whispered. "Go into the house. Perhaps they will not pass this way."

"They will pass this way," said Dominic grimly, snatching up his clothes. "As I follow the Firebird, so they follow me."

"Quick!" she pleaded. "Go into the house before you are seen."

"What about you?"

She gave him a bitter smile. "Why should they trouble to hurt a simple woman of the Forest who does not have the gift of heresy? I have nothing better to do than bathe in the pool and bask in the afternoon sunlight. Now go!"

Axe, Sword, Mace, Lance

Dominic ran up the grassy bank and into the tumbledown house. He threw his clothes on quickly and had just finished when the Four Horsemen came slowly round the edge of the pool. In his haste, Dominic had left the door open. It was too late to close it now. He stood back in the shadow and watched.

The woman was sitting unconcernedly upon the grass with her long dark hair spread loosely over her shoulders as if she was still waiting for it to dry. The Four Horsemen, their mail and silver masks glinting with the sun's reflected fire, drew up in front of her.

"In the name of the Inquisitors, greetings," said the Sword.

"There is heresy abroad," said the Lance. "Therefore we pursue it."

"One, touched by the flame, who sees that which may not be seen, has entered the Forest," said the Mace. "Know you, woman, of such a one?"

"The Forest is wide," she answered. "I have seen no man this day—touched by the flame or not."

"Did we then speak of a man?" enquired the Axe softly.

She looked startled for a moment, but recovered herself.

"It is men chiefly who traffic in heresy," she retorted. "Women have no taste for such matters."

The Four Horsemen somehow appeared to regard her more intently, though no eyes could be seen behind the narrow slits in their silver masks.

"You are naked," observed the Sword. "It is heretical to display the body without shame."

"Until you came," she said, "there was none to see my nakedness. I have bathed in the pool and the sun has dried my hair. And by your leave, I will presently put on my clothes."

"You have lain here on the grass, woman?" asked the Lance.

"That is so."

"And yet," thundered the Mace, "there is the impress of two bodies—two bodies, I say, locked together in lust and vileness and deceit!"

From inside the tumbledown house, Dominic saw that the woman was now half crouching in terror.

"Harlot!" roared the Axe, towering above her. "Liar! You have defied the Four Horsemen." Slowly he raised his weapon.

Dominic could endure no more. With a cry of rage, he rushed from the house, and in one great leap, flung himself bodily at the grim figure. His attack caught the Horseman by surprise. Its impact toppled him from the saddle so that he fell heavily to earth. Before he could recover, Dominic, already springing forward again, snatched the battle-axe from a mailed hand and brought it crashing down upon the silver mask still almost at his feet. Without pausing to see the effect, he grasped the terrified woman by her arm and threw her behind him. Then he whirled to face the three remaining Horsemen.

He was surprised to find that they were still watching impassively, while the riderless horse trotted slowly away into the Forest.

"Well met, heretic!" said the Sword. "Now you shall surely die."

Dominic swung the great axe round his head so that it whistled through the air. A tremendous power seemed to be rising in him. He was invincible. No one, he felt, could stand against him.

"I am touched by the flame," he taunted. "I have seen that which may not be seen. I have seen the glory of the Firebird, and I shall follow it always . . . Come! Destroy me before heresy spreads through the land. Destroy me—if you can!"

Without answering the Sword turned away, allowing his horse to move slowly along the edge of the pool; and the two remaining Horsemen followed him. But when he had gone a short distance he turned suddenly, and then the earth shook with the thunder of his charge.

One after another they came, their weapons high and bright and menacing, as if the weight of the charge itself would hurl Dominic into oblivion.

"Die, heretic!" screamed the Sword. But even as he struck, a heavy blow from the battle-axe almost passed through his body and he fell with a gasp from the rearing horse.

There was no time to look, no time to think, no time to decide. Dominic leapt nimbly away from the riderless horse just as the Mace came upon him. He sensed rather than saw the terrible blow that was about to be delivered to his head; and then the axe whirled high, and the mailed arm wielding that heavy spiked weapon was severed at the shoulder.

The Lance came on.

Dominic saw that its bright point was aimed steadily at his chest. It did not seem possible that such an attack with such a weapon could be broken. And yet . . .

And yet it had to be broken!

In desperation, and with all the strength he possessed, Dominic hurled the axe from him. It seemed to fly almost along the shaft of the lance. There was a great cry as its blade struck the Horseman full in the chest.

For a moment, Dominic thought he had failed. Somehow the Lance managed to keep to his saddle and came on. But his weapon sagged, and the point buried itself in the earth, swinging the shaft up with such force that both horse and rider were overthrown.

The panicking horse struggled quickly to its feet, trampling its rider heavily. Then it swung round, cantering after the others into the Forest.

Suddenly, there seemed to be a stillness.

Dominic looked at the woman. Now that the struggle was over, there was time to think, time to remember. It seemed impossible that one could have stood against four—four who were armed and armoured, and on horseback.

"I have destroyed them," he murmured wonderingly. "Alone, I have destroyed them!"

She was still trembling. The terror had gone from her eyes but she was still trembling. "Have you?" she said sadly. "Look at what you have destroyed."

The mailed figures lay inert and sprawling as they had fallen. There was an emptiness, a flat and curious deadness about them that was more grotesque, more strange than death itself. One of them lay on his back —a crushed and oddly shrunken heap of armour with the silver mask turned blindly towards the sky.

Dominic went to the figure and knelt by it. There was something about the posture that was utterly macabre. He studied it for a few moments, then suddenly tugged at the enigmatic mask. It came away easily and revealed—nothing.

There was no face behind the mask, no body in the armour. No vestige of anything human.

Only emptiness.

The shock of discovery was more dreadful than the shock of battle. He had stood against four ruthless pursuers and had destroyed them. He had fought victoriously against four hollow enemies.

The woman came to his side. Dominic stood up and held her close, feeling the need to reassure himself of some reality, feeling a great need to experience the closeness of the living.

"So you have destroyed nothing," she whispered. "They were never alive and so can never be killed. That is the nature of the Four Horsemen. They are immortal in their very lack of substance. They are tireless even in their lack of physical power. They are invulnerable and invincible." She paused, shivering. "Their names are Distrust, Fear, Hatred and Envy. And they will pursue you for ever."

But Dominic was hardly aware of her words; for there, against the dark background of trees, hovered the Firebird. Its subtle, shimmering radiance transforming the whole scene—the pool, the tumbledown house, the four mailed figures at his feet and even the dark-haired woman by his side—into a living tableau of gold.

There was music in the air and in his limbs. Music and power and purpose. The Firebird rose slightly, and an invisible cord pulled at Dominic while the power danced through his body.

"What is it?" whispered the woman. "What is it, my dear one? There is such a light in your eyes, such a darkness and a mystery and a burning vision that my heart grows cold—I know not whether with joy or despair. What is it, my only love?" She held closer to him as if, instinctively, she realized that he was already going from her.

"I can see the Firebird," he answered softly. "It calls and I must follow."

"If only I, too, could follow!" She clung desperately to him and gazed at his face as if she would memorize every single line—as if she would engrave his features in her heart.

But Dominic was no longer looking at her. He was no longer aware of her loveliness or the subtle warmth and pressure of her body against his. The Firebird seemed to be commanding him entirely. His eyes were fixed upon the burning wings, the body of pure flame. Once more the invisible cord pulled at him.

"Goodbye, my dear and lovely one," he murmured in a distant voice. "I will remember the way our bodies played and the way our hearts were moved. I will remember our love throughout the rest of my life."

The Firebird circled almost impatiently, and the cord pulled tight.

"Pray that I have conceived," she cried, feeling the power that seemed to be physically tearing him from her arms. "Oh, pray that I have conceived!"

Suddenly, the Firebird began to glide towards the trees. And, at the same moment, Dominic was free and away. His limbs were light and his body was filled with energy. He leapt forward in pursuit of the Firebird and did not look back.

Yet Still He Ran

In a few moments he was surrounded by the gloom of the Forest once more. The trees rose high and motionless, their thick roof of intertwined branches and leaves shutting out the intensity of the late sunlight. But Dominic was untroubled either by the darkness or the brooding atmosphere; for the Firebird was there, wheeling and gliding between the trunks of trees, leading the way and annihilating the gloom with radiance wherever it passed.

On and on ran Dominic, his eyes fixed always upon the dazzling creature of flame with its slow, stately wingbeats and its bright, purposeful beauty. On and on through the Forest. The pace was becoming faster now, but Dominic felt no fatigue. The thorns and undergrowth tore at him, the bole shoots of trees seemed to whip at his body as he passed; but he was heedless of the pain and his feet hardly seemed to touch the earth.

On and on. The passing trees became giant columns of blackness receding faster and faster on either side as he sped after the fiery vision that danced always ahead.

Then, suddenly, Dominic passed out of the vault

of darkness into the vaulted freedom of the open sky; and the Forest was behind him.

Higher and faster soared the Firebird, sending great ripples of energy along the invisible cord. Faster and yet faster ran Dominic, exulting in the sheer joy of pursuit, as if he, too, had wings and would presently rise into the sky.

And as he ran, his shadow ran before him—long and lean in the low-slanting sunlight. A giant's shadow taking gigantic strides across heath and grassland and marsh, crossing gullies and streams in grotesque leaps, twisting and dancing and gliding over the uneven ground.

Time was meaningless. As he followed the hypnotic creature, the bird of fire and beauty and purpose, Dominic knew that he had engaged in a race that could never be won—a race with eternity. But the knowledge was irrelevant. All that mattered was that he should follow the Firebird whenever he found it and wherever it led—even to the end of his life.

Time was meaningless, yet the cavorting shadow before him grew longer and longer, stretching and rippling and reaching out like a thin mobile strand that, presently, would draw itself out to infinity.

Dominic had eyes for nothing but the Firebird. He might have been running over mountains and valleys, he might have been passing through arid deserts or sweet-smelling flower gardens, and he would not have known. He knew only that there was pattern and purpose in the journey, that this alone was enough.

The pursuit became a dream, and the dream was unending—until, abruptly, the shimmering creature of flame swept low before him in a wide circle, then soared almost vertically with such speed that it became transformed into an arrow of fire . . .

And vanished.

Dominic stopped running. He stood bewildered.

The air was still, the sky was a quiet, deepening blue; and it was as if the Firebird had never existed.

He stood bewildered; for there before him, some little way ahead, lay the City, its smooth wall gold and crimson in the rays of the sinking sun. He saw that he was standing on the road between the City and the Temple. Suddenly he was aware of a great fatigue.

The tiredness seemed to course through his body like a gentle acid, dissolving his muscles, softening his bones, eating through his will to move.

He looked at the City once more. Towers and spires and domes and high roofs were visible above the crimson wall. They seemed to be beckoning him, offering visions of rest, of peace and forgetfulness. There was a single broad gateway in the City wall. Slowly, painfully, he began to walk towards it.

Each footstep was a tremendous effort, an individual triumph. As he hobbled towards the City gate, Dominic let his mind dwell on that incredible pursuit of the Firebird. It did not seem possible that, so recently, he could have displayed such singlemindedness and put out such immense energy for a pursuit that had always ended and would always end in the same mysterious way.

One moment the Firebird was suddenly there, giving him such courage, such faith and fixity that nothing could deter him from its pursuit. For a while, he would be godlike, invincible. He would cross the world with giant strides until—until, inexplicably, the Firebird disappeared once more just as mysteriously and unexpectedly as when it chose to appear. And then he would be alone again—alone and perplexed in a world that he would never truly understand. Dominic wondered how much of his life he had already given to the journey—and was oddly consoled by the knowledge that, in the end, he could only give it all.

He became aware of an unmistakable throbbing in the ground. He looked up in surprise and bewilderment. There at the City gates the sun's low rays glinted on four advancing shapes—the indestructible Horsemen. They slowed down and finally became motionless as if they were waiting for him; as if they knew that, more than anything now, he wanted peace and rest and an escape from his loneliness in the nearness of men. They were waiting for him, their silver masks glowing like embers in the red light of the sun. They waited as if they knew that, at last, he would come to them.

Dominic realized that he was almost spent. Defeat was there at the City gates—defeat and comfort and rest—waiting only for his acceptance. He took one more step forward and sighed, knowing that if he surrendered himself to the ways and customs and laws of other men he would never again see the Firebird, never again taste the lonely joy of unending pursuit.

He took another step and then another; but the ache in his heart became greater than the ache in his limbs. He stopped.

And knew that there was something within that could never accept defeat.

Slowly, and after some hesitation, he turned from the waiting Horsemen and looked back along the road towards the lowering sun. There in the distance rose a tall, familiar landmark whose roof seemed to support the great fiery ball.

Perhaps, if he could reach the Temple, he would be able to escape.

If he could reach the Temple.

Dominic put one foot forward, and instantly heard the subdued thunder of hooves behind him.

His spirit sent urgent commands to his weary limbs—commands that seemed to travel with leaden slowness along a burnt out filigree of nerves.

He began to run. He looked down at his legs in sheer amazement. It did not seem possible that limbs so tired and worn could obey him. Their very obedience seemed to renew his strength.

He ran painfully and with stumbling strides along the road to the Temple, remembering the speed and ease with which he had pursued the Firebird, and hoping that he would see its glorious life-giving shape once more.

Behind him the thunder of hooves was louder. The road seemed to be trembling under his feet.

Dominic glanced over his shoulder. The Horsemen were gaining rapidly, their weapons raised high, their masks glinting with malevolent intensity. He looked resolutely ahead. The Temple still seemed far away, and he knew that he could never reach it.

But still he ran.

Pain danced crazily along his limbs. There was a roaring as of great waters in his head; and mists of darkness threatened the blurred power of seeing in his eyes. Yet still he ran.

The thunder of the hooves seemed all about him, filling the earth and the sky, beating their dreadful rhythm of emptiness and despair throughout the world.

The chase was a nightmare—a purgatory of tortured limbs and bursting lungs and heartbeats that threatened to tear his chest to pieces with their violence. The chase was a nightmare, but the night-mare was real.

And thunder rolled around him like a gathering tide of destruction. For the Four Horsemen were almost upon him. But there at the end of the road ahead—so near now and so hopelessly far—lay the broad steps of the Temple. They seemed to ripple at him strangely, tantalizingly, through waves of darkness; and he knew that both the darkness and the Horsemen were closing in.

A Ripple of Eternity

Then suddenly there was light.

Light and radiance shimmering in the Temple itself. Dominic knew with a great surge of joy that the Firebird was waiting.

There it hovered between the great columns of marble that seemed, in the intense radiance, to be themselves shafts of living fire.

Dominic goaded his limbs to a tremendous effort. The presence of the Firebird drew him; but there was no longer the pull of that invisible life-giving cord, there was no longer the surge of god-like strength. He was completely exhausted, yet he willed himself forward in a final agonizing drive to the Temple. As he half fell on to the smooth steps, the thunder at his heels died abruptly into silence. He turned in surprise and saw that the roadway behind him was entirely deserted. The Four Horsemen were nowhere to be seen. It was as if, in reaching the Temple, he had somehow accomplished their disintegration.

He lay there on the steps resting for a few moments, allowing his poor hard-driven limbs a brief respite after their long endurance. Presently the tearing sharpness in his chest became dulled, and the pain in his legs began to die into a curious numbness. He lifted his head and looked up the broad flight of steps.

The Firebird still hovered, waiting.

He gazed at it, forgetting his weariness and the great sense of desolation that had tormented him. The fiery shape no longer seemed to be filled with violence and power. The character of its beauty was dominated now by a serene stillness, a frozen tranquillity that seemed to inspire a sensation deeper and calmer even than peace.

Dominic got to his feet and slowly ascended the steps. He was no longer conscious of his body. He felt, indeed, that he no longer possessed a body, that he was no more substantial than a dream, a whisper or a legend.

Slowly, the Firebird circled the Temple, then hovered for a moment on the tip of the high crystal cone that imprisoned a slender tongue of blue and yellow flame. From the tip of the cone it drifted gently down to the transparent sphere containing a single red rose. And from the sphere, the Firebird slowly passed through the circular opening in the Temple's polished floor.

As Dominic watched, he remembered his first vision of the cone, the sphere and the Temple in the bright and early glory of morning. It seemed so long ago now—so long ago that perhaps it, too, was nothing more than part of an inconsequential dream.

Moving with trance-like deliberation, Dominic went to the opening and lowered himself through it. The radiance of the Firebird filled the subterranean passage; but, strangely, he did not need to look for footholds on the uneven rockface. He seemed now to be floating, drifting inevitably towards the hypnotic creature of flame and mystery.

The Firebird was gliding along the rough passage; and Dominic, too, was gliding—drifting without effort in pursuit of the unattainable.

On went the burning and dazzling shape, and on went Dominic. Already they had reached the great dome cavern where the Firebird had carved the air into a tracery of flame as it danced with indescribable beauty. Again, as they passed through the cavern, the Firebird was dancing. But this time it was a dance of stillness. A dance of tranquillity and peace.

Dominic was closer now to the Firebird than he had ever been. Drifting along in a timeless dream of movement without motion, he felt that it would be possible at last to reach out and touch the fiery wings, to let the elixir of warmth and life flow into him in the moment of mystical contact.

But he did not desire to touch. He wanted only to follow, to offer the devotion of silence—a great and abstract love, the detachment of complete submission.

Now they had left the cavern and had once more entered the narrow tunnel that led to the folly. The long journey, Dominic realized, had resolved itself into a circle. It had started at the beginning, and its end would still be a beginning. But there was purpose in retracing the last steps. There was pattern and purpose and music in the mysterious dance of life.

His re-emergence in the tiny stone folly took Dominic by surprise. Still following the Firebird, he seemed to glide without any exertion up the stone steps of the bower—back into the world of reality. An ordinary sunset world slipping quietly into the ordinary stillness of an ordinary evening.

But perhaps that, too, was part of the great illusion. Perhaps this world was no more real than the one to which his pursuit of the Firebird had led him. Or perhaps neither had anything to do with reality at all.

Dominic stood in the folly and watched the Firebird float delicately over the lake towards a sun that was already sinking below the distant edge of the world. He stood for a moment, savouring the quiet glory of the landscape.

Beyond the thick belt of trees along the bank of the lake was the house where he had been born. A house that, even if he returned to it, could now only be filled with ghosts and memories—even if the ghosts were encased in flesh and the memories draped with texture and colour. And there, hidden in the woods, was the ruined cottage with its strange and wonderful door—the door he had had to open.

He remembered that far away dawn adventure with gladness. There were no regrets.

The Firebird was no longer drifting low across the still surface of the lake. It was beginning to soar up to the crimson-streaked reaches of the sky. Perhaps, thought Dominic, watching its ascent with a calmness that seemed to bubble inside him, it will rise to join the stars. And then he began to wonder if, perhaps, the Firebird itself was a star—a star that belonged to him alone. As he turned the possibility over in his mind, he automatically walked to where he had left the small boat that very morning—or perhaps it was a thousand years ago.

Presently, he found himself drifting upon the surface of the lake, still watching the slow, stately soaring of the Firebird. Now, it was no more than a brilliant point—a tiny golden spark set like a jewel in the deepening sky.

So this, he thought peacefully, is the end of the journey. He was both joyful and sad. He had seen much that was strange and wonderful, but he had achieved nothing. And yet—and yet the journey was its own fulfilment. And the challenge of the journey was all.

But it was not quite the end.

Suddenly the needle-point of fire began to grow. It grew quickly and beautifully into a great arc of flame as the Firebird swooped, illuminating the whole world with its transient light. Down it came; and it seemed to Dominic that the bright talisman of fire would pass straight through him. For surely nothing could halt such a self-consuming fall.

It was over in an instant.

Without creating even a tremble on the surface, the Firebird passed deep into the waters of the lake.

Dominic gazed down where it had fallen. There was no trace at all of that blinding radiance, that wonderful fiery plumage.

But illuminated by the last rays of the setting sun, he saw his own face. He saw the thin and wrinkled features, the white hair and still bright eyes of an old man.

He gazed at it for a moment without either surprise or regret. Then with a great sigh of contentment he sank back into the tiny boat. For an instant only, his body became taut with all the magnificent purity and power of fire. Then it slackened as his spirit was borne outwards on a tiny, tremendous ripple of eternity.

And then there was nothing but the darkness of night, the remote compassion of the stars.

From the
World's End

To
JUNE

I cannot seek the Golden Fleece for you,
    Nor fight strong Brecca all a winter's day;
Nor find that tree from whence the Phœnix flew
    Above the Well of Life which, far away,
    Springs from the world's confines. No longer may
These old romantic deeds reveal how true
    Our constancy of love; the beasts we slay
Quest not as once made plain to mortal view.

Yet in dim woods the Golden Bough still grows,
    And Dragons lurk, and pale Morgana sings—
Woods of your heart and mine: and through the night
Of half-seen shapes it leads where, shining bright,
    Dwells our true Phœnix with immortal wings
Guarding within our hearts the Singing Rose.

CONTENTS

Into the Valley

... He reached the level land ...
Then looked and saw, near by, on his left hand
An old house, folded round with billowy piles
Of dark yew hedge. The moss was on the tiles,
The pigeons in the yard, and in the tower
A clock that had no hands and told no hour.

Dymer: C. S. LEWIS.

It was later than either Julian or Rosanthe intended when they came out from the tall, quiet ruins of Valle Crucis Abbey in the Valley of Llangollen, and strolled together up the rough farm-track towards the main road where they had left Julian's car. The heavy shadows cast by the old trees in the intense August sunlight lay deeply across the white dust, and seemed to surge against their legs like the shallow waves on a level, sandy beach; and the drowsy silence, made living by the indistinguishable murmur of bird and bee, was broken only by the lowing of a cow in the long grey buildings to their right.

Rosanthe kicked at the dust with a little restless movement of her feet, and shook back her hair.

"How cold and dead it was in the abbey," she said abruptly. "I hate abbeys; they always seem full of death."

"Ruins certainly can be depressing," agreed Julian rather lamely, not following Rosanthe's drift of thought, yet anxious to agree with her wherever possible.

"But there must have been plenty of life there once—before the monks were all turned out, and the buildings destroyed."

"Oh, monks!"—Rosanthe seemed determined to be difficult—"they would have made it even deader than it is. A lot of unnatural old men pottering about in the twilight, and mumbling prayers to a God they had forgotten how to believe in when they forgot how to live!"

"I certainly hold no brief for monks," agreed Julian, this time with conviction, and looking with altogether unmonkish eyes upon the girl who strode along so freely and so full of life beside him. "But if one had been—well, unfortunate," Julian articulated the words with a shade of embarrassment, "unfortunate in the things of life—well, I can imagine few better places to which one could retire than the peace and tranquillity of an old monastery."

"Yes, and what an old fossil you would be!" interrupted Rosanthe, "worse than an Oxford don! Julian, you really are the limit: you've a one-track mind, or something; whatever one says, you will always drift drearily back to the same subject—the forbidden subject, remember!"

"I'm sorry," said Julian contritely, "I didn't intend it: only it's a subject that everything appears to lead to these days. And the strange peace and spiritual repose which the abbey seemed to hold and pour over one rather accentuated it—that's all."

"The abbey was merely morbid and damp," corrected Rosanthe with far too much energy to believe what she said. But she did not pursue the subject, for this was indeed dangerous ground, and it was that knowledge and the fay quality, which—though she would never have admitted it to Julian—the abbey had imparted to her also, that made her so anxious to return to what she would have called the world of reality with as big a bump of temperament as she could muster.

In silence they came out on to the main road, where the tar seemed to shimmer and dance in little curls of smoke a few inches above the surface as it curved away over a low rise in the road before them.

Julian's little old two-seater car slanted up the grass verge to one side, and releasing the brake, he pushed it easily down on to the road before holding open the door for Rosanthe. They were still silent as they went forward at a brisk pace, in and out of the shadows as the road wound and climbed up the long valley.

The sun was very near the hills behind them when Julian brought the car to a standstill near to a narrow turning on the right which led at a steep angle down a lane into the valley bottom.

"What have you stopped for?" asked Rosanthe dreamily. The evening light on the hills and trees across the valley, and the listless feeling that the dusty day was drawing to a close, seemed to have fallen over her during the last silent half-hour, and she turned almost gently towards Julian as she asked the question.

"This is the way to Eclwyseg," he answered, speaking also in a hushed voice as if not to disturb the peace of the evening. "You remember: the little road up into the mountains which that funny old man at Dinas Bran Castle said was called The World's End?"

"He said there was a house up there, which no one visited," Rosanthe murmured, "and beyond the house you came to the end of the world, and could go no farther. Yes, I remember; and he said something in Welsh which neither of us could understand."

"It almost sounded like a blessing, didn't it?" Julian took up the recollection thoughtfully, "and he looked as if he ought to have been the last of the Druids. Funny old stick, I wonder who he was?"

"And wasn't he interested and impressed when you told him that your ancestors used to live at Dinas Bran!" Rosanthe went on. "That's when he told us we ought to go to Eclwyseg, wasn't it? Yes, and he seemed so eager that we should go. . . . I wonder why?"

"Well, if we want to go to Eclwyseg, now's the time," interrupted Julian.

"Shall we go?"

"It rests with you entirely."

"Have we got time?"

"Yes. It doesn't matter if we get to Chester after dark."

"If we are too late, my grandmother will get worried."

"Oh, we won't be very late."

"She'll think you've abducted me."

"I wish I dared!"

"I'd like to see you try!"

"Well, what about Eclwyseg? We can't stop in the middle of the main road much longer."

"Do you want to go?"

"Oh yes, I want to go. Very much. Very much indeed."

Rosanthe ran her fingers up and down the narrow

gold chain round her neck. What were these odd thoughts that were chasing each other backwards and forwards across her mind? Sometimes they came out clearly into her consciousness, but more often they lurked just out of sight—fascinating, enthralling, and just a little bit frightening. . . . Something seemed to be calling her towards Eclwyseg, calling almost with music—calling until the golden light and the green leaves swam before her eyes, and were drowned in strange, unintended tears. . . . And something rose up against her and drove her back from Eclwyseg: almost a visible form, like a cold dark shadow, with half-seen hands which pressed against her bosom until she could scarcely breathe. . . . What did it mean? For a moment she was in a waking nightmare, struggling to remember half-forgotten things—struggling at the very fulcrum point between the two decisions. . . .

And then Julian began to quote poetry in a low voice:

> Out of the silence and the shade
>> What is the voice of strange command
> Calling you still, as friend calls friend
>> With love that cannot brook delay,
> To rise and follow the ways that wend
>> Over the hills and far away.

With a little suppressed gasp, as if cold water had suddenly been flung into her face, Rosanthe recovered from that strange moment—woke up from the filmy edge of sleep which had claimed her for a little space of time.

"Let's go to Eclwyseg," she said decidedly, and as the car slid easily down the narrow hill and on between the tall green hedges, she sang, hardly knowing what she did, a song that Julian had written for her:

> Into the shadows falling
>   About the dying day
> We wander: voices calling
>   Tell the way.
>
> The mountain shadows bending
>   Their heads as if to pray
> Call to us at the ending
>   Of the day.
>
> And there, no longer lonely,
>   Your hand in mine, we stray
> Through all the worlds—ours only—
>   Far away.

How long they went forward into the evening neither of them could remember: the long, kindly shadows seemed to close about them and blunt the edge of reality. They went on as if half asleep, as if waking and dreaming had become one state—just as day and night had become one in the gold and shadow of the evening.

In front of them the low hills rose into mountain fastnesses, the dark fir trees clustering up their sides until they ended in the bare grey rock of the cliff summits. The higher mountains were on the right, sheer bastions of prehistoric rock rising like the walls and towers of a titanic castle built in primeval ages by the race of giants. To the left was a lower grass-covered ridge coming in before them and sweeping up through the trees that almost blocked the head of the valley, into a great and mysterious pass which led only into an unknown darkness.

Down in the valley itself the trees clustered thicker and thicker, and the hedge beside the road gave way to moss-covered stone-walls, laid cunningly together without the use of mortar; and in time the walls ceased also, and the sweet-smelling pine woods came down to the very roadside, and arched darkly over the narrow track.

Before long it ceased to be a metalled road; the stones gave way to fir-cones that crackled audibly beneath the wheels, and the white dust was replaced by pine-needles and soft, springy earth. Presently the track, which had run nearly on a level for some distance, began to rise and wind in and out among the trees, running beside and occasionally through the mountain stream which came leaping down the valley. It skirted from time to time about great grey out-croppings of rock from which the lichen hung in festoons, and the heather filled every lap and fissue of the stone, like pools and rills of purple wine.

And then the car stopped, quite suddenly, and without any jar. The engine raced for a moment, muttered brokenly, and choked into silence.

"Hallo, what's wrong?" asked Rosanthe as if waking from a half-slumber. And her voice broke into a great silence which had not been stirred by the purr and rustle of the car.

"I don't know," said Julian, appealing in vain to the self-starter. After a few unavailing efforts, he got out, opened the bonnet, and groped among the half-visible mass of metal entrails, but without result.

"We can't have run out of petrol; I had five gallons put in at Llangollen; and we haven't done more than twenty miles since then," he remarked as he checked the petrol and oil gauges.

Rosanthe had got out and was watching Julian's unexpert tinkerings.

"Do you understand anything about the inside of cars?" she asked rather anxiously.

"Not very much, I'm afraid," he admitted; and a quarter of an hour's strenuous toil failed to rouse the faintest sign of life from the engine.

From time to time Rosanthe attempted to assist Julian; but as neither of them knew much about the mechanism of a car, assistance tended to become interference and advice seemed always to be criticism or even recrimination; and before they gave up in despair the tempers of both had become frayed to a far greater degree than the occasion warranted.

Finally Rosanthe, who was nearly crying with annoyance—she hardly knew why—remarked to Julian in a voice as cold and neutral as she could make it: "What on earth do we do now?"

And Julian, far more hurt than either the words or the tone of her voice could normally account for, replied, in much the same key: "I suppose we'd better go on, and see if we can get help. We've no idea what's wrong with the car, and we've come at least twelve miles since we left the main road, without sighting a single house; but from the look of the hills when last I could see them, I think that we must be fairly near the beginning of the pass, and so we should not be far from the house the man at Dinas Bran told us about, Eclwyseg Manor, where the descendants of the old Princes of Wales found refuge after Dinas Bran was destroyed. But, of course, if you have any other suggestion——"

"Hm'm!" said Rosanthe, still very much put out, "to look for this wretched house does seem the only thing to do."

Julian nodded agreement; and when they had pushed the car a little way under the trees to the left of the road, they started on up the gradual slope, walking briskly with the whole width of the track between them.

The road curved onwards into the shadows, winding a little more steeply towards the grey shoulders of the pass which were visible from time to time, now on one side and now on the other. As they walked, the evening drew in closely about them, slanting steep swords of soft caressing gold between the dark tops of the fir trees, and here and there across the road where the night was already gathering like a dark river. The birds grew drowsy and murmured away into silence; the last pheasant coughed and chuckled sleepily and was still, while an owl woke and wailed in the distance, and the rabbits thumped lazily away as the sunlight faded from the open hillside.

Neither Rosanthe nor Julian could ever understand or disentangle the strange medley of emotions and conflicting sensations which surged about and between them during that strange walk.

Beside the car they had both experienced and been submerged by a sudden wave of the petty, irresponsible annoyance of spoilt children; all the more disconcerting because it had found no expression in words. But now the brooding peace of that deep, ancient wood and the lovely, undefinable tranquillity of evening seemed to be filling them, seemed to be purging away the strange access of childish petulance, just as the long, smooth waves of the incoming sea dim, and cover, and forget the medley of uneasy tracks and footprints on a sandy shore.

They walked at first on either side of the road, silent, defiant and supremely independent. A glance stolen across by one to the other was, if intercepted, broken off with an abrupt turn of the head, accentuated by a momentary nonchalance in the walk, a scornful curve of the shoulders. As the path wound up the valley and grew steeper and narrower, so they drew closer together: but they did not look at each other, nor make any movement of reconciliation.

The sensation of a sudden calm after a tempest, the almost choking inrush of physical and spiritual well-being that comes when acute pain is suddenly terminated, fell upon each of them as they came unexpectedly round a corner between two out-croppings of rock and found themselves clear of the wood and walking upon the soft, short grass of a clearing where tall trees grew sparsely, making of it a stretch of miniature park-land hewn from the solid jungle of dark fir trees.

The darkness was gathering fast about them, welling up from the ground like silent, clinging mist; but the glow of evening still lit the gently sloping park-land. It dripped in flakes of crimson light from the wide leaves of chestnut and oak; it shone back from the polished foliage of the laurels which clustered tall and thick about a house beyond the park: a silent, ghostly house of grey stone topped with white plaster set unevenly between dark beams beneath a heavy roof of thatch and tiles grown over with lichen and wild flowers. The sunset flamed back from the leaded diamond panes in the narrow windows, but there did not seem to be any light from within.

Julian and Rosanthe advanced slowly towards the house, following a path which wandered among the trees. It led them a little to the left, round about a clump of laurels, and suddenly into a sunk knot-garden with crazy-paved ways winding among the box-hedged flower beds to a grey sundial three steps up in the centre.

As they drew near to the sundial both Julian and

Rosanthe realised that they were now walking hand in hand, though neither had any recollection of when this had begun. They stood together on the second step, and Julian read out in a hushed voice the legend carved on the stone round about the lead dial: "Time Trieth Troth."

At another time Rosanthe would have scoffed at so much-used and trite an inscription, but now she did not even loose Julian's hand, though she felt his fingers tremble and grow tense about her own. Indeed, as they passed on round the plinth of the sundial and continued their course towards an arch in the yew hedge through which the house glimmered faintly, she drew even closer to him until his arm slipped under the crook of her elbow.

Out of the knot-garden they went, and up four wide, shallow steps on to a grass-grown terrace extending round the corner of the house, which they could now see was of considerable size and shaped like the letter L.

Walking along the end of the house, they tried to look in through the two windows which came to within a foot of the ground, but it was so dark inside that it was not even possible to tell whether the rooms were furnished or empty.

"Let's go round to the front," suggested Rosanthe, also speaking almost in a whisper. "I'm sure someone must live here—the garden is so well kept."

At the corner they found themselves at the upper extremity of the short line of the L, looking along it to the angle where the main ascender branched off. This, the real front of the house, was heavily grown with Virginia creeper and wisteria, except for the low wooden porch over which clung and dropped great sprays of white roses that glimmered in the semidarkness.

The longer grass across the front of the house appeared black like deep, stagnant water, and it struck a sudden chill to Rosanthe, whose bare feet, protected only by sandals, felt the tingling cold of fresh dew.

She clung suddenly closer to Julian, welcoming the arm which he placed around her and the firm pressure of his fingers on the curve of her waist.

They came to the door in silence, and paused before it. The last ray of sunlight broke suddenly through the horizon clouds across the bottom of the valley, away behind the hills which fringe the Dee beyond Llangollen; it cut like a sword through a gap in the surrounding trees and rested on an engraved plaque of tooled lead which was set prominently in the triangular space made by the beams above the porch, and Julian read out the words which were engraved there in great clear letters— letters of dull fire in that strange light:

"Ovner na wyr ovn," Julian pronounced slowly, his voice trembling suddenly and growing deeper as the meaning of the sentence came home to him.

"Well?" asked Rosanthe, catching something of the awe from his voice.

"It's Welsh," said Julian, "it means *Let him who has no fear, fear here.*" The beam of light died out as suddenly as it had come, and with it the letters of the inscription faded and disappeared into the grey shadow above the wooden architrave of the porch. Julian and Rosanthe stood quite still and silent for a long time; and the darkness of night came about them, the sombre blue of the sky turned into black, drawing the first stars away into infinity and leaving the two alone with the chill fear of solitude, of being the sole tenants of a silent and forgotten planet.

With a sudden effort, but without withdrawing his

arm from Rosanthe's waist, Julian stepped into the
blackness of the porch and knocked at the door with
a great ring-knocker of iron which swung there; and
the sound echoed and reverberated through the house
like the thunder of ocean waves in a deep cave.

The House of Fear

The shadows dance upon the wall,
    By the still dancing fire-flames made;
'And now they slumber, moveless all!
    And now they melt to one deep shade!
But not from me shall this mild darkness steal thee:
I dream thee with mine eyes, and at my heart I feel thee!
    A Day Dream: SAMUEL TAYLOR COLERIDGE.

"It's empty," whispered Rosanthe, "quite empty and uninhabited. . . . But how strange that the garden is kept so beautifully, and the outside of the house is in such perfect repair. Knock again, Julian, as hard as you can!"

Julian did so, but still in vain. "There's no handle on the door," he said, "or at least I can't feel one. What shall we do?" He took a cigarette-lighter out of his pocket as he spoke, and struck a light which filled the narrow porch with yellow radiance. The door was of dark wood, blackened by age, studded with nails and traversed by wrought-iron hinges. The ring of the knocker was set in the mouth of a great carved head nearly two feet in diameter in the centre of the door. . . .

"My God!" said Julian, and he dropped the lighter, which instantly went out. But Rosanthe screamed—which was a thing that she could never remember having done before—and the two of them clung together like frightened children.

"It's . . . it's only a carved metal face," said Julian at last; but his voice was still trembling as he added hysterically: "It is the eye of childhood that fears a painted devil." What shall we do now? . . . There *isn't* a handle—and I didn't notice even a keyhole. . . ."

"Don't let go of me, Julian!" Rosanthe's voice broke in a strangled sob, and she clung to him, trembling. "Don't let me see it again. . . . I didn't know there could be anything so horrid in all the world. . . . Julian, this isn't real, is it? It's a dream, a nightmare, surely?"

"I . . . I don't think it's a dream," said Julian, "I'm *sure* it isn't a dream. But it's . . . it's . . . well, it's odd," he concluded lamely, for what he felt could not be put into words. "It's like a waking dream—or like being very much wider awake than ever before. . . ."

"But why are we so frightened?" asked Rosanthe, who that morning would have sacrificed anything rather than admit to fear. "I mean to say—well, it *is* only a carved face. But there's more than that: the atmosphere is terrifying—the house is terrifying. . . . If I believed in ghosts, I should say that there was a particularly evil one haunting this place. But that's nonsense. Only . . . I'm so frightened, Julian. It's like being a child again, lost in the dark, certain that *something* was getting ready to jump out at one—a ghost or a tiger, that didn't make any difference. . . . Only now it's a much bigger fear."

"Yes, dear, I understand," said Julian, his arm

tightening a little round Rosanthe's shoulders. "To me it's like one's first sight of violent and unlovely death—or one's very first experience of ungoverned passions. . . . But it's only an iron knocker on the door of an empty house. . . . And it's our house in a way, Rosanthe—or mine at least—if I really am descended from jolly old Roderic Mawr and company! Look, there's nothing to be afraid of here— and I'm going to knock again."

As he spoke, he seized the ring in his right hand and raised it on high to strike even harder than before. But as he did so, it turned sideways in his grasp; there was the click of a well-oiled latch, and the door swung silently inwards, revealing a large and dimly lighted hall, panelled in dark wood, and flagged with red sandstone.

There was no one in sight, and only the echoes replied when Julian summoned up sufficient courage to shout: "Is anyone there?"

"Let's go in, Julian," said Rosanthe, "it has become so cold outside, and it looks warm and inviting in the house. And I'm sure that whoever lives here will not blame us—for we did knock as hard as we could."

Together they stepped across the raised threshold and down two steps into the room, the door swinging shut behind them with a muffled crash.

Julian led Rosanthe across the hall to where a great log fire burned richly in a large metal fire-basket under a wide chimney-piece. In front of the hearth was a shaggy lion-skin rug, and on it two tall, straight-backed chairs, seated with interwoven strips of wide brown leather. There was a table also, set a little away from the chairs, and yet sufficiently between them to be within convenient reach of either, and on the table a meal was laid for two persons.

"If we stand by the fire and wait for a few minutes, someone is sure to come for supper," said Rosanthe looking rather longingly at the table. She put her hand on the silver lid of one of the vegetable dishes, and drew it back quickly. "Yes, at least some of the food is hot, so they won't leave it for long. Let's get warm while we're waiting."

Rosanthe settled herself down on the hearth-rug with her hands held out to the blaze, while Julian stood with one hand on the mantel-shelf above his head, leaning a little inwards to the fire.

Neither of them spoke for some time, and the house was filled with silence broken only by the rustle and catch of the flames in the dry wood, and an occasional whistling choke as the fire opened a seam in an old log where a vein of sap still lingered.

What they were thinking about neither could have described. After the sudden, unreasoning terror in the porch, a heavy peace seemed to have descended on them both—a numbness of mind growing with the increasing bodily comfort. But in a little while the ascendancy of physical sensations began to make plain to both of them that they were exceedingly hungry—and that a tempting and appetising meal was spread out within their reach.

Rosanthe rose slowly from before the hearth and turned to look at the table. The three candles set in a silver candelabra behind the white cloth burned steadily and brightly, reflecting back in the silver dish-covers and cutlery. Two empty plates were set on Rosanthe's side, as if ready for her to fill, and in front of the plates was a great pewter dish on which rested a cold sirloin of roast beef. By each place was a heavy silver tankard and a delicately cut wine-glass, and to the side were bottles of red wine and a tall earthen flagon of ale.

Rosanthe seated herself at the table with a sudden defiant movement. "Come and sit down, Julian," she said, "and we'll begin before the vegetables get cold." She picked up the horn-handled carving knife and with great determination cut two large slices from the "under-cut" of the joint, put them on the top plate, and handed it across to Julian, who had by now taken his place at the other side of the table. He raised the lids of the two silver vegetable dishes and held them while Rosanthe piled their plates with baked potatoes and chopped carrots, and then, taking a liberal spoonful of horse-radish sauce out of a silver sauce-boat, he pushed it across to her, and fell to without a word.

They both ate in complete silence, speech having ceased to be a necessity to them, and drank freely from the earthenware jug, and afterwards from one of the wine-bottles which Julian uncorked. And when the meal was ended, Rosanthe returned to the hearth-rug, where she sprawled not too elegantly, with her head against one leg of the chair.

Julian, after opening the second wine bottle and helping himself liberally from it, lowered himself a little unsteadily on to the rug beside her and rested his head against her shoulder.

"I feel better now," he said thickly, "warm and comfortable, particularly comfortable."

"Me too," assented Rosanthe, leaning back a little so that Julian's face slid from her shoulder to her breast. "So warm and comfortable, warm and comfortable. . . ." Her voice trailed off inarticulately.

Julian put his arms round her and drew her clumsily towards him, muttering thickly. If his strangely bemused mind had sent any conscious thoughts to leave his lips in words, it was "I love you, Rosanthe"; but the declaration that actually took form was of a cruder and coarser texture, to which she replied in similar phrase. Soon he crushed her savagely to him, and her holding back was a bidding rather than a denying. Then he kissed her with a sudden fierce curling of the lips: and at that moment the Fear fell between them like a sword of cold night air in the fetid heat of the room. For an instant, a fraction of a second more infinitely smaller than a second of light, as her eyes looked into his and his into hers, each saw the other's face twist and curl into a terrible living identity with that other face, the face on the knocker of the House of Fear. Then, as they drew apart with a mutual cry, they were looking into each other's faces once more—the two frightened children who had clung together for protection from the sudden, unknown terror which had been so apparent before they entered the house.

"What was it? My God, what was it?" gasped Rosanthe, shivering and trembling in spite of the warmth of the fire.

Julian shook too: he turned his head from side to side and moved his shoulders uncomfortably.

"Rosanthe," he began, stumbling and hesitating for words, "I'm awfully sorry; I . . . I don't know what came over me, I. . . ."

"It's all right," she interrupted gently, laying her hand on his, "I was just the same—it's not your fault —nor mine either. I just felt as if—as if there was no mind, no reason left in me, only impulse, physical impulse. Ever since we began to eat—since we stood by the fire even. Oh, Julian, I'm so frightened again. Where are we? What is this house that we have come to so strangely?"

"We are in Eclwyseg Manor," he said, trying painfully hard to speak in the slightly pedantic style that was a favourite pose of his—"the seat of the descendants of the old Princes of Wales. But—but I don't know really where we are at all, any more than you do. And I can't explain our—what just happened —in the slightest. It was as if one had lost one's soul —as if one had become a beast, a beast prowling outside the sheepfold, one of the 'kin of Cain,' like Grendel in the poem. But the 'why' of anything is quite beyond me!"

"You know that I don't believe in the things that you do," she said, but with none of the violent dogmatism of the unconvinced. "And yet— and yet —Julian, if I ever could believe in souls and redemptions and things like that, I'd believe in them here. I'll admit at once that whatever you believe is really genuine to you—so tell me honestly, please, do you think this house is haunted?"

Julian laughed a little, but Rosanthe could understand that there was no grain of mockery in it; "You do put things so firmly," he said, his forehead puckered in perplexity, "and I can't possibly in this instance give a straight answer to a straight question. I think that there are spiritual forces moving round about us, moving in us too, the whole time: I'd rather not speak of angels and devils, for the words have been vulgarised out of all meaning years ago. You only admit mind and body into our make-up; I add a third member to the trinity—the soul—and believe it to be the ultimate whole. . . . Oh damn the English language—I can't explain a bit what I mean, but sound merely like a rather dogmatising lay preacher! Never mind. . . . But I think that the spiritual world has invaded the physical with rather less camouflage than usual—and for some unknown reason we are in the centre of the battlefield—or the battlefield is in the centre of us—it makes very little difference. Sorry, my dear, I wish you wouldn't get me on to metaphysics; I know none of the proper jargon, and anyhow I expect that my personal views must seem pretty nonsensical to anyone else."

Rosanthe moved restlessly. "You don't think the food might have been drugged?" she suggested.

"An aphrodisiac, or something?" queried Julian with a slight smile, "I suppose that is the only explanation left to the materialist! It seems wildly improbable—though this whole business is quite beyond any ordinary experience!"

A peaceful drowsiness now began to steal upon them—very different from the sensual coma which had been theirs after the meal. When the conversation started, both had been determined to discuss the situation fully and from every angle, but now the need for discussion seemed to have drifted away; wonder remained and was powerfully present, but curiosity faded and ceased almost to make itself felt.

The fire, which before had crackled and blazed with some animation, had burnt down to a comfortable red glow, and the candles in the room behind them flamed steadily and unwinking.

The fear had quite faded from both Julian and Rosanthe, just as their previous experience had in its turn been banished by the fear and was now an unimaginable state and not part of them at all.

"I wish there were some books here," murmured Rosanthe, the cynical pose of the twentieth-century girl quite forgotten under the new influence which was stealing around them like subconscious music. "I'd like you to read to me. Some old story— *Aucassin and Nicolete,* or Malory, or something out of *The Earthly Paradise;* I haven't read them for years. Julian, you read those kind of things, can't you remember one story—in nearly the proper words?"

Julian had been about to suggest some such scheme himself: "Poetry," he said, almost under his breath. " 'Following darkness like a dream'—I could say *La Belle Dame Sans Merci,* or *Love,* or *The Blessed Damozel;* or tell you the story of one of the great romances: the Argonauts, or the Volsungs—or something more recent, *The Sundering Flood,* or *Lilith, Aylwin* or *Perelandra* . . . or something like this," and he began to speak, almost as if in a dream, the words falling into verse, without any will of his own, just as the figures and fancies in his memory took on a dim, mysterious shape in the red heart of the fire and among the glimmering shadows on the grey stone wall of the ingle-niche:

> "Who would hark to an old lay?"
> In a land of poplars grey
> Nicolete is wandering,
> Where the flowers lie thick in spring. ...
>   Green leaves over the forest glade
> Shadow where our hearts have strayed,
> Dreaming under summer skies,
> Dreaming till the visions rise,
> We may see but cannot hold—
> Dream awhile the Age of Gold:
> Rosalind among the trees
> Of Arden. . . . By the Grecian seas
> Helen, wandering with pain,
> "Till Odysseus come again". . . .
>   In the rocks where heather red
> Bleeds beneath the golden head
> Of English gorse—there Lorna calls. ...
>   By the mist-hid waterfalls,
> Summit grey and curlews crying,

Lost to sight, to love undying,
Winifred shall wander still.
    And upon the purple hill
High above the dreaming sea
Miriam shall ride with me.

There was a little silence when Julian ceased speaking, and again to both of them came the ghost of a distant music and a picture of the places where beauty dwells in its true blend of sight and association: the long vista of a valley in Greece, temple ruins among silver olive trees and a shepherd's pipe far away above the frowning bastions of Parnassus; the red wall of an old garden half-hidden by shrubs and climbing roses, and beyond it the creeper-covered house amid green lawns and knotted oaks; a river in late Spring seen from a punt, with willows drooping into the water, and grey towers, murmurous with bells, half-visible across meadows. . . . And when Rosanthe spoke, it was to follow on the "unpremeditated art" of Julian's words:

Calling, calling down the forest glade
    Of Arden in the Spring:
Seek me, ah seek me there, the fairest maid
    That youth or dreams might bring.
    Follow . . . following
    Love on the bird's wing,
    Still where the shadows fall
    On the grey college wall
    Where you sit alone. . . .
    White rose on the grey stone
    Where the meadow breathes of hay. . . .
    Faintly from far away
    The murmur of to-day,
    Down by the Cherwell stream—

But lost like a dawn dream. . . .
Faintly the broken chime
Of bells mourning for time,
Bells that stir tears
Down the dim years
Like a voice breaking in grief. . . .
Summer calls: flower and leaf,
Fritillaries like wood smoke
Under the green oak
Where stand slow cows. . . .
White still the chestnut boughs,
But the breeze passing by
Brings snow from a clear sky. . . .

The music playing behind Julian's consciousness as Rosanthe ended seemed sunk and swollen to the deepest notes of some grey organ in a great, dim cathedral where massive Norman pillars towered to an invisible roof and the evening sunlight turned the glorious colours of a Burne-Jones window to a scene in some dimly imagined paradise.

And now Rosanthe had risen to her feet, the candles on the table making a halo of her hair, her eyes wide and shining in the firelight, her lips parted as the music surged through her also. Julian was kneeling before her, and his voice throbbed with emotion as he spoke:

Rosanthe—day-star—at your feet I feel
As though I were some pilgrim fain to kneel
In some dim abbey at the cloudy shrine
Of a virgin saint: the coloured sunbeams twine
In opal and blue and crimson on the stone,
Channelling down the dark lines in old brasses,
Where they fall from the rich windows. Priests intone
Like the murmuring understream where a river glasses

The sweet choir-voices of far-distant birds;
While the slow organ breathes to blur their words,
Making sound cling with the incense . . . kneeling there
That pilgrim feels the saint bend to his prayer—
Bent and incarnate, till her hands are spread
In healing benediction over his head. . . .

    To you, Rosanthe, I thus long to kneel
In worship of my saint, whose power to heal
Fills all my wounded spirit full with awe,
The wanderer's peace who finds his native shore
After uneasy danger of the sea.
Rosanthe, goddess of my life and me,
Surely such love transcends all base desire—
Eternal calm outliving lust's brief fire. . . .

Julian ceased speaking and raised his eyes to Rosanthe's. Very slowly she bent down towards him, laying her hands first on his head and then on his shoulders: both were trembling, but with the ecstasy of worship. Near she drew and nearer until, as if in some sacramental act of oblation, her lips touched his brow. And then the fear fell between them like a fierce beam of tropical sunlight cutting through the sepulchral chill that a moment before seemed to be spreading in the room. And again for an undefinable fraction of time they saw each other horribly changed, found themselves looking into empty eye-sockets hollowed in a dead, grey face: but the face was still in some horrible, indescribably way the face on the knocker of the House of Fear.

Two frightened children, they stood clinging to corners of the chair-back in front of the fire.

"Look here, Julian," said Rosanthe rather unsteadily, "whether it's the food, or the wine or some poisonous herb burning in the fire—or whether it's a . . . a gaggle of ghosts having a scrap round us (or in us, if you like)—I can't stand this any longer. And, whether the house is inhabited or not—I'm going to bed! Suppose you take one of the candlesticks, and lead the way up the stairs: then if there *are* any ghosts, you can deal with them!"

"Righto!" assented Julian, his jauntiness as laboured as her matter-of-factness, "the only ghost in an old barrack like this would be a Poltergeist—and they are usually rats, anyhow. An irate owner is much more of a danger, but never mind. 'We lack the season of all natures, sleep.' Come on!"

He seized a candlestick and passed it to Rosanthe, took another in his left hand, grasped with his right the hand which she held out to him, and they began to walk slowly across the room to where a wide wooden staircase with dark Laud bannisters extended a little way into the room before it disappeared between panelled walls in the direction of the main part of the house.

The Voices in the Mist

For she set her hand to the fire,
   With her mouth she kindled the same,
As the mouth of a flute player,
So was the mouth of her;
With the might of her strong desire
   She blew the breath of the flame.

> *Atalanta in Calydon:*
> ALGERNON CHARLES SWINBURNE.

There was no breath of wind on the staircase, nor down the passage which Julian and Rosanthe found stretching ahead of them as they came up out of the dining-hall in the manor of Eclwyseg; and the candles which each held aloft in their triple candlesticks burnt clearly and steadily. At the top of the long flight they paused to look about, and found themselves in a fairly large room which extended from side to side of the house across the head of the staircase. Two passages went from it immediately to right and left behind them, and the one straight, wide corridor opposite; and the candle-flames reflected from the dark diamond-paned windows on either side. The room was, again, walled with dark oak, but here were set painted panels both round the room and down the corridor; dim, discoloured representations of men and women in every period of dress back even to a time that showed traces of the Roman influence which must have died later in Wales than in the eastern parts of England where the Saxon power was sooner felt. Upon each picture a name was written, and Julian read out the old curled letters of those to either side of the corridor:

"Cadwan, Cadwallo, Cadwallader" to the left, "Nest, Mervyn, Roderic Mawr" to the right, and in the alcove where the corridor began, and where one picture was set on a slight curve at each side, "Owen and Angarhed. . . . The ancient kings of Wales . . . but I thought that most of them were mythical—remember the skull of Cadwallader in *Headlong Hall*? There was a Roderic Mawr right enough, and he died in 876; and Owen and Angarhed joined the two rival houses of Powys and Gwynydd. But if there was ever such a person as Cadwan, he would have lived early in the seventh century: the legends would make him some relation to King Arthur—or at least to Uther Pendragon—and a descendant of the Ancient British kings, Cymbeline and Caradoc—if not Ferrex and King Leir. And if any of these old coves are genuine, they're all my ancestors—how jolly!"

Julian's rather lame attempt at jocularity was not needed, for the atmosphere of the House was fast undermining the last traces of Rosanthe's scorn for things romantic and sentiments outmoded.

"There's something frightening in the feeling of so much time," she said, half to herself, "a sort of responsibility, an obligation—but one that is pleasant to bear."

Julian laughed quietly: "It's odd how people nowadays hate the idea of loyalty or obligation," he said, holding the candles up before the portrait of Angarhed. "But these—these ancestors give one a much bigger feeling of the legacy of life, of its seriousness, anyhow. . . . Yes, it's odd to feel that her blood flows in my veins . . . Angarhed: she was alive a thousand years ago—up at Dinas Bran, I expect. She married her cousin, Owen. . . . A thousand years ago. . . . He might have fought at Brunan-burh—at least one Welsh king was defeated by Æthelstan, and the place isn't far from here, if we accept the site in Wirral. . . . Oh, hang it all! It's something much bigger than 'Old, unhappy, far-off things, and battles long ago'—but there doesn't seem to be any way of explaining it. Perhaps it's only false sentiment; yet it *does* have an effect. Think that Owen and Angarhed were once just our age—a thousand years ago—and wandered hand in hand up this same valley, seeking like us for the World's End. . . . I'm sorry, my dear—that sort of thing 'gets' me awfully, you know: and it's not the same for you."

Rosanthe did not speak, but her hand seemed to say many things as it trembled in Julian's—only neither of them had as yet much knowledge of this the oldest and subtlest of all languages. But they began to walk slowly down the passage, pausing every now and then to look at one of the picture panels which were set regularly between the many doors on either side. As they advanced the costumes advanced with them through the ages, but the pictures did not appear to grow any newer, and the names continued to be single Christian names, the women on Rosanthe's side and the men on Julian's. On, still on they went—Caroline, Restoration, Queen Anne, Georgian, Regency, Early Victorian, Late Victorian, Edwardian—and then they came to the end of the passage where two doors confronted them, set each at an angle of forty-five degrees from the wall so that they shared a common door-post in the centre of the passage.

As they paused before these doors and held the candles on high, a little exclamation of surprise or fear broke from each of them—for the highly polished wood of the doors gave back a perfect reflection in the same dim and misty colours as the portraits.

"That gave me quite a shock!" said Rosanthe, raising and lowering the candlestick to make sure that her reflection did likewise. "But however odd this house is, I don't really think there's anything supernatural about it."

"Look back along the passage," said Julian quietly. Rosanthe turned with a little intake of breath—but the passage was empty and pitchy black.

"It's quite dark," Rosanthe objected, a touch of irritation in her voice.

"Exactly," said Julian, "but there was a bright fire and at least a dozen or more candles burning happily in the entrance hall when we left it: there is no turn in the stairs, which are dead opposite the end of this completely straight corridor—but there's not a glimmer of light. How do you explain that?"

"I don't," said Rosanthe, and with sudden determination she turned the handle of the door in front of her, and pushed the door open.

Here another surprise awaited them, for the room within was lit by a bright fire on the hearth; the curtains of faded tapestry were drawn across the windows; a bed, the foot of which was immediately opposite the door, was freshly made up, with the white sheets turned down ready for an occupant.

Rosanthe stopped just inside the door, looking about her uncertainly.

"It almost seems to have been got ready for me, doesn't it?" she said. "Have a look next door, Julian, and see if it is ready for you." Julian did as she suggested: "Yes," he said, "this room is the exact duplicate of yours, and prepared in the same way."

"Well, then," declared Rosanthe with decision, "I'm going to bed in mine immediately—and you'd better do the same."

"You think you'll be all right alone there?" returned Julian.

"Of course I will," exclaimed Rosanthe indignantly. "I'm neither a child nor a Victorian miss—and I'm certainly not going to invite you to come and look after me. . . . If the ghosts get too importunate, I'll knock on the wall—there seems to be only a thin partition between us."

"My bed is on the other side of the same wall," assented Julian. "Good night—and pleasant dreams."

"I don't dream," said Rosanthee laconically, ignoring the hand which Julian half held out to her; "Good night," and she shut the door with a bang. With a shrug and a sigh he went into his own room, closing the door none too gently either, and began to relieve his feelings by poking the fire with some violence.

Why the hell did Rosanthe suffer a change of mood every few minutes? he asked himself. What had he said or done to offend her? Really, it was a bit thick; she was quite old enough to behave better; did women never know their own minds from one moment to the next? . . . Julian's vindictive manipulation of the poker ceased abruptly, and he sat on the wooden stool by the fire, gazing into vacancy and smiling ruefully to—and rather at—himself.

With a shrug and a grimace he got up and went over to the window, where he drew back the curtain and opened the narrow leaded frame. He leaned out into the night, breathing in the cool air until the blood tingled in his veins. All outside was very dark, for the moon had not yet risen, but the sky was powdered with stars, and he could see the vast mass of the hills as black holes in the shining fretwork. He could dimly make out the ground slanting up steeply to his left as if the house grew right out of it, for he perceived that his room and Rosanthe's were situated at the extremity of the main mass of Eclwyseg Manor.

Feeling strangely revived and tranquil, Julian shut the window and, without removing more than his shoes and jacket, flung himself on the bed, lying on his back with his head turned a little inwards to the room. As he drowsed there in the kindly glow of the fire and candles, he presently perceived a book on the table beside him, and reaching out an idle hand he picked it up and fell to examining it.

The binding was of old leather, engraved on back and front, the one side with a rose, which he thought idly must have been the crest of the Tudor descendants of the old Welsh Princes; but on the other side was a bird which could not, he felt, be other than a Phœnix though, unlike the usual modern pictures of the Arabian bird, it had its wings folded to its sides, its head thrown back as if in song, and the flames from its nest rising high on either side of it like ghostly arms, which seemed to hold above its head what might have been a cloud of smoke, a halo, or even a crown of thorns.

Turning to the first page of the book, he found that it was an illuminated manuscript, but apparently of recent execution, and written upon paper. There was no title-page, nor any indication of date, and it seemed to be unfinished, for there was no colophon, and the last quarter of the book consisted of blank leaves, the contents, which was in verse, breaking off in the middle of a word.

Opening it at random, and turning the pages aimlessly, Julian began to read:

Then Launcelot said: "I must go forth again,
Though witting well of dangers by the way;
For all too long has pined the fair Elaine
In prison cold unvisited of day."

And forth did Launcelot in shining mail
Betake him to the perils of the wild:
Threading each lonely moor, each silent dale,
All unafraid—by sin yet undefiled;

Until he came upon the eventide
Where a grim castle loomed above the glen;
Nor might he on his journey further ride,
For there dwelt wights, the wickedest of men.

Quoth then the knight to those who barred his way:
"Fair sirs, I prithee stay me not this tide,
For I must hence, and that without delay,
Nor fain am I to turn me now aside.

In a high castle, held of caitiffs vile
My lady lies; and I am come abroad
To seek her in this land of snares and guile,
And leave her path to freedom with my sword."

As he read, the room seemed to slip away; the walls grew farther and farther apart, the light faded into a glowing mist that hid all from him but the little space immediately beside the bed, and there seemed on a sudden to be figures moving in that mist, a pageant of great themes which he could not see, though a vague, intangible knowledge of their meaning came through to him.

The book fell from his hands and he lay back, dimly conscious that he neither slept nor was awake.

As he looked, the gleaming mist drew together until in the twilight he could see three very shadowy shapes, but as yet he could make out little of figure or face except that all three of them were women. But as they grew more distinct, he became aware of a distant humming sound which developed in a little while to a strange music: hardly a music as we usually know that art—for this was a concord of sounds rather than a series of notes and harmonies: there was the rising and falling moan of the wind among lonely mountain fastnesses; the tinkle and splash of a continuous waterfall; the indistinguishable murmur of birds and bees in a summer garden; sea waves booming on a cavernous beach, and sea waves sliding away down a sloping shore and drawing a myriad pebbles slipping wetly over each other with a mushing sound like a long, quivering sigh. And these were only the themes and overtones of the music: underlying all were deep chords that vibrated through Julian until he knew their origin and yet had no finite thought or word to say whence they came; and there were bars and passages without number, trills and quavers in the music, which caught and held for a moment tantalising echoes of belief and experience.

But the music faded when the figures in the mist began to speak, though for a little while Julian could not tell which it was who spoke, nor any particular difference in their voices. But one said, almost as a continuance of the music for there was no jar at the beginning of her words:

In man's heart many things are set
To remember, to forget.
The ages are his: all the past
Through him like a tempest blast
Passes, leaving dust behind—
Star-dust to waken, earth-dust to blind.

The last word drifted on with the music, and was
caught up by another voice, clearer and higher than
the last:

Blind. . . . So blind in the world's light,
Lost in valleys of the night:
Man groping all his days,
Seeking by dim ways,
Seeking for peace. . . . Blind, blind:
What rest may his soul find?

And the deeper voice seemed in reply:

He shall find rest in strife;
Beyond war peace abides,
Through pain the gate of life,
In pain life hides. . . .
Out of sorrow is joy born,
Darkness and light are one:
Man from the womb is torn,
From night the sun.

At which the clear, high voice, shriller and more
heart-piercing than before, broke in:

Ah, cruel is my flesh like fangs,
Yet no wolf rends me now:
There are pain-drops on my brow,
In my heart pangs of joy. . . .

The voice faded away in a cry of indistinguishable pain and rejoicing which was taken up by the music which rose and swelled in heavy organ tones, until it died away leaving the three voices speaking together in solemn chorus:

> We who were old when the world was made,
> Who still shall be young when the earth passes,
> Speak to the heart of a man afraid
> Of his unknown life: in his heart that glasses
> Dreams of the child bred out of dim memories
> Born of dead men who have dreamed as he;
> Young in the life that was old to them, or is
> New as the sun to the ancient sea.
> Long remembered and long forgotten,
> Dreams of a boy who must dream alone:
> Shapes in his heart that are unbegotten,
> Living gods and unbreathing stone.
> Man who is one and alone, though many,
> We in your heart, to your hand the world,
> Show the form of a Quest: not any
> Pageant of kings by the dawn unfurl'd
> With robes of gold and with wrath of nations;
> But a half-blurred cut by an unskilled hand,
> Poorly inked, as are heart's creations,
> Clumsily struck, by a burning brand
> Of strife and pain for a half-dreamed glory
> Of lust below and of life above:
> The world in your heart a realm of story,
> The heart in this world an unfound love.

Julian was sitting up now, his head against the wooden partition wall that separated him from Rosanthe. He felt no surprise at the strange scene before him, but a certain sense of unreality—rather as if the three figures in the mist were actors performing a morality play for him and for him alone. But just as he had come to this conclusion, the nearest of the three stepped slowly out of the shadow into the bright circle of candle-light and came and stood beside the bed.

He could see her now quite clearly: a tall, finely formed woman with long golden hair and a face of quiet, statuesque beauty. She laid one hand on his, and he felt that it was cool and steady. The touch thrilled him, but with an exaltation that had no trace in it of sensual pleasure or expectation: it was the thrill of a solemn music heard on a cold night, or of a wide seascape with stars seen alone.

"Julian," she said, and her voice was very clear and silver-toned, but cold, beautiful and remote—a voice that made him think of water dripping into a still pool among the grey rocks of Mereion: only in this pool the cold star-reflections were unstirred by the ripple of the falling drops:

"Julian, you are very welcome here to my dwelling-place. If you will come with me into the night and follow where I lead you, all shall be made plain between the call of the heavens and the clutch of the earth; and you who follow a dream shall find its coming like a star of pure worship."

"Lady," said Julian, afraid, he hardly knew why nor of what, "how can I come with you and follow what you seem to show? I do not seek for any star, but simply, as we all do, for what I believe to be the greatest happiness and the fullest life—which for me is centred in and through my love for Rosanthe. But I remember a dream of love . . . was it a dream, or is it the highest truth? . . . Love separated from all that is vile and common and sordid . . . a worship wherein man is all spirit as God is a Spirit, and the flesh, which is the Devil's gift, is purged away. . . ."

Julian had begun to speak with a certain knowledge of his own clearly held beliefs—beliefs that had come to him very recently and indistinctly, but with a grasp at truth that he had never before experienced: but now as he spoke, the fear of doubt fell upon him, and with the doubt a return of the horror, which much lonely conflict towards a way of life had for long left with him, of the frankly physical in the human relationships all around him.

The cool hand rested still on his own, deadening the life in him, and after a little silence the voice spoke again, but more urgently and compellingly, though still utterly dispassionate:

> Think not of the world, awhile
> Set around us to beguile,
> Nay, but harken and forget. . . .
> Youth and Spring together met
> In a garden of old time,
> In a season sweet with rhyme,
> In the Bower of the Rose
> Where the fragrant walls enclose,
> Stagnant in a sea of strife,
> Youth's bright mirror of his life:
> Spring with Youth together weaving
> Shades in shadowy attire,
> Till the world fades from you, leaving
> Ghosts of unassuaged desire.
> Know the world as you would dream it,
> Meet with life where no life is:
> Woo the shadows that beteem it,
> Shadows fading from your kiss.

Suddenly there was feeling in her voice, but the sense was one of fear, as of a dark shadow falling over her

words and compelling a meaning which she did not
intend, but was powerless to expel.

Julian drew back as he saw her cringe away, and
he heard a low musical laugh, very different from the
first, though a girl's voice also: there was a compelling huskiness in it, a warmth as of a Summer
wind across a green bank where violets grew under
the shadow of the chestnut leaves; it seemed to draw
him out of the great windy places into a warm garden
of sleep where the sweetness of the flowers was always about to become too sweet, yet never cloyed.
Looking up he saw a dark-haired girl, slim and
active, but well formed, with a bright, open face,
large eyes that were laughing and yet languorous,
just as her lips were firm and yet sensuous. In striking
contrast to her companion who was dressed in full
and flowing robes of white, she wore completely
modern attire—a short, pleated skirt and a short-
sleeved white cotton blouse well open at the neck.

She put her hand on Julian's, and the blood surged
hotly through him at the warmth and firmness of her
touch.

"Who are you?" he asked, drawing away a little,
but without loosing her hand. "You come like a
shadow darkening a field that shines with dew in the
early morning. Do not come any nearer, you are
frighteningly strong. . . ."

"Cast off her hand, Julian," said the first lady,
"she is the snake, whereas I am the star. Follow me,
Julian, and I will show you the true world. She will
deceive you, for no man can withstand her once he
has taken her by the hand."

The girl laughed again pleasantly: "Don't listen to
Astrid," she said, "for Astrid, though a dear girl in
her way, is a complete reactionary." Then with a

sudden change of tone, and leaning nearer and nearer
to Julian as she spoke:

> Ah, man, you call me shadow,
> Black on the dawn meadow;
> Nightshade among celandine:
> Yes, but warm lips are mine,
> Soft arms that call to you
> As the sun calls the dew.
> In your heart I awake
> And my way take,
> Though you call me Snake
> And dream of a Star!
> Julian, such dream hands are
> Vain comfort for the shrill
> Cry of the world's long ill. . . .
> Come, for I call you now:
> The fruit grows rich on the bough,
> The sap grows fierce in the tree,
> And Spring down the green lea
> Calls to the poppy-shade. . . .
> Spring is too long a maid. . . .

She ended almost in a whisper, bending over Julian
so that the sweet fragrance of her and the warmth of
her breath were all about him, stirring and madding
his senses until he stretched impetuous arms to crush
her to him. But she drew away suddenly, one finger
to her lips; and Julian, he knew not why, sank back
on the pillow with all continuance of intellect and
emotion suspended. He lay back in the stillness of the
room, in the utter stillness that followed on the voice
of her who was named Rhoda; and very faintly,
beyond the distance and across many worlds, he
seemed to hear another voice speaking or singing.
Whether it came from the third shadowy figure in the

heart of the golden mist he might not know; at first
it was so faint he could scarcely tell that there was
indeed a voice; it was so remote that there seemed
nothing in the world to which he might liken it. For a
moment the clear drops of water fell into the pool of
unwinking stars; for a moment the languorous wind
murmured huskily above the violets and among the
roses in the still garden. But the voice held far
deeper and more wonderful images behind these—
vistas of music and the sweet sadness of poetry; dim
shapes of that eternity which no human mind can
imagine; the cry of deep seas beyond whose fear is
the joy of harmony; the murmur of Rosanthe's voice
that grew to an infinite softness about his name; the
sudden shadow of peace falling with the pale light
upon the bowed worshipper in a little Saxon church:
images merging and blending into one another, the
rival lores of Astrid and Rhoda grown to a single
harmony about the unformed words of the third
voice, until the three voices came to him as one
voice—the voice of Rosanthe singing:

> Here in the shadows of man's knowing,
>   Beyond the shades eternally,
> 'And through the world, a bright shape going,
>   Still in the heart the heart of me.
>
> Here in the world to eyes scarce seeing
>   Hid and revealed in your desire,
> Ghost of the peace that still is fleeing
>   Eternal fledgeling of the fire.
>
> Here in the heart for ever dwelling,
>   Lost in the heart that seeks me there;
> Flesh of your flesh by flesh compelling,
>   Yet must Ixion clasp the air.

Here in your form my form completing,
   Your subject and your deity,
Still through the world a bright shape fleeting,
   Seek in your heart the heart of me.

While the voice spoke to him Julian was held, it seemed to him, in a cyclone centre of complete peace; but the song brought with it a sensation and a longing of the aspiration and endeavour beyond peace. For a little while his mind was clear as it had never been before, and he understood the truths after which he had groped for so long—though the understanding faded into the dim, tantalising recollection of a half-remembered dream before the song had ended.

But when the last notes had died away, he sprang to his feet, pushing Astrid and Rhoda aside, and crying out loudly: "Rosanthe!"

And then, as the mist cleared suddenly from the room and he stood alone in the centre of the floor, he heard Rosanthe's voice cry out as in an access of fear:

"Julian! Julian! Help me! Oh, Julian!"

In a moment he was out in the passage: her door was wide open, and he leaped into the room.

The candles still burned in their silver sockets, and the fire glowed amiably on the hearth; but the bedclothes trailed on the floor in wild confusion—and Rosanthe was gone.

The Unsubstantial Pageant

My brain is wild, my breath comes quick,
    The blood is listening in my frame,
And thronging shadows, fast and thick,
Fall on my overflowing eyes;
    My heart is quivering like a flame.
To Constantia Singing: PERCY BYSSHE SHELLEY.

When Rosanthe parted from Julian at the door
of her room she felt vaguely and unreasonably angry
with him, though she could not decide exactly what
he had said to annoy her. She sat by the fire for
some time, nursing one knee and staring into the
flames: Julian was a bit of a problem, certainly—and
he gave himself such airs! Or did he just say the
wrong thing completely unaware of its natural effect
on her? Julian. . . . Rosanthe's mind played round
him in intricate circles, pleasure and irritation inextricably interwoven as she thought. And with his
image came the recollection of their strange experiences in the dining-hall as they sat by the great
fire; she tried to remember what exactly had happened, and to account for it if she could; but her
recollections kept becoming blurred so that she could

135

no longer distinguish the actual events from the general vague knowledge of her own and Julian's natural reactions. Julian's natural reactions . . . and surely he had tried to kiss her . . . surely she hadn't allowed that . . . and then she saw in a dim corner of her mind the likeness of the face on the knocker. But she brushed aside the recollection fiercely, almost shaking herself as she rose to her feet, and walked over to the window which she opened, and leaned out into the pleasant summer night.

She had almost forgotten that it was summer: the fires in every room in the house and the heavy curtains had conjured up a subconscious picture of wintry landscapes and biting frost. But the moon slipping a silver sword between the horizon clouds glimmered on full foliaged trees, and upon flowers on the lawn which sloped up past her window, rising steeply to where great cliffs blotted out the night. There was a soft breeze blowing which caressed the curls on her forehead, and a distant music might have been a nightingale even so far north as Flintshire.

More at peace with herself, Rosanthe closed the window and returned slowly to the bed. After a moment's thought, she took off her shoes and unfastened her skirt, but lay down fully dressed on the outside of the clothes, only drawing the coverlet over her bare legs, and tucking it in round her waist.

She lay back for some time staring at the ceiling, which was ornamented with Tudor Roses formed in the plaster, and a pleasant drowsiness began to steal over her in which her thoughts seemed to move and inform without the conscious direction of her mind. They were oddly clear and distinct, yet impossible to recapture the moment they were past: only she knew that Julian was playing a far-too-prominent part in them, and with a sudden effort she pushed his image aside and turned her attention rather violently into other channels.

And as she lay, striving to picture her own life, a future bright and hard as a diamond, real and actual as sand-polished steel, there came an unexpected sound which did not interrupt the silence nor break the flow of her thoughts—a gentle knock on the door.

Rosanthe did not know whether she actually said "Come in," for the will to say it seemed no sooner to be formed before the door opened softly, and a girl of about her own age entered the room. In an odd fashion Rosanthe knew the girl already; she had no recollection of meeting her before, though she realised that she might well have done so, either at Oxford or in the "Bohemian" circles on the fringes of which she had moved a little in London. The girl was slightly formed and looked delicate, though her strong, full movements disproved any such impression; she wore blue velvet slacks, a short-sleeved yellow aertex shirt open at the neck, and a wide brown belt round her waist. Her hair hung rather lankly to the level of her chin, but was smartly groomed none the less, and nature was well counterfeited in her complexion though rather exaggerated in the excessive carmine of her lips.

"Hallo!" she said in a clear, rather listless voice, striding over to Rosanthe and seating herself on the foot of the bed, "I'm Rosamund. Have a smoke." She pulled a packet of cigarettes out of a pocket and flung one to Rosanthe, setting another between her own lips, and striking a match on the heel of her shoe. She did not offer a light to Rosanthe, who leaned over the table to the nearest candle-flame. In doing so she knocked off a book which had lain on the table-edge, but caught and held it with a quick automatic movement.

"Pretty lousy dump, this," continued Rosamund, "you must be quite browned off all alone here. . . ."

"Well, there's Julian," hesitated Rosanthe.

"What, the guy next door?" interrupted Rosamund scornfully, "I shouldn't think he was much better than nothing—absolute drip, I should say—and not your type at all: positively reactionary, if you ask me—wants to get back to nice, comfortable Victorianism, buy a wishy-washy little miss out of a schoolroom, and show off his superior manhood before her adoring eye through years and years of complacent married life. I know his sort—won't have a good time himself, and doesn't want anyone else to, particularly if it's a woman—wants a housekeeper by day and a tart every night, isn't man enough to pay for them, so gets married. Well, never mind him—he won't give you any fun. Have a drink?"

Rosamund stubbed out the crimson-ringed butt of her cigarette on the carpet and strolled across to a cupboard in the wall from which she took glasses and a couple of bottles. She filled the glasses and returned with them, setting one on the table beside Rosanthe and sipping the other herself.

"I don't think Julian's as self-satisfied and old-fashioned as all that," Rosanthe began slowly, "though he has certainly a lot of the absurdest ideas . . . particularly about love and marriage——"

"Twin souls, love eternal, marriages made in Heaven," interrupted Rosamund again, not hiding a yawn, "I know the jargon—it's a stale line. Oh, look here, Rosanthe, cut it out! You're modern, you're a realist, you've outgrown all those medieval superstitions and taboos: forget about him and all the tiresome things he stands for; come and have a good time with me; see the world, and experience it, too —we only live once!"

"There's a lot in what you say," agreed Rosanthe, "and one grows old so horribly soon: there really *is* no reason, is there, why we should look ahead more than a year or two? Why shouldn't we get what happiness we can out of life—particularly these days when the future is so uncertain. . . ? But Julian believes in things like an after-life, and . . . and I don't know quite what——"

"Oh, let him, if he likes," Rosamund interrupted again, draining her glass and rising to refill it and Rosanthe's, "it's this life that matters, if you ask me. But I suppose he's got to be awfully good here, to qualify for a nice, comfortable seat in some mythical Heaven. Let him, if it amuses him, but don't allow him to muck up your life for you."

"That's not at all Julian's attitude," said Rosanthe, toying nervously with the book which in the interest of the conversation she had forgotten to replace on the table. "He's quite a realist in some ways, but he doesn't think that romanticism is all escapism and reactionary superstition. And—and I like Julian, better than any man I've ever met," she ended a bit lamely.

Rosamund yawned. "Oh, well, if he has that sort of effect on you, go to bed with him by all means— you'll soon get tired of each other when the excitement and novelty of that wears off. But in the meantime, enjoy yourself: meet people—hundreds of people—nothing so fascinating as people, if you don't know any of them too well. Come on, drink up! Life's so much easier when one's just floating nicely. . . . Look, I've got some friends waiting outside—may I bring them in?"

And without waiting for a reply, she went over to

the door and, opening it a little way, began to hold a low-voiced conversation with someone outside.

Rosanthe drew her legs up a little, a sudden shiver of cold going over her, though the room was rather warmer than was comfortable. The fire still burned redly, and the candles on the table beside her lit the part of the room near the bed with a pleasantly soft glow, leaving most of the rest in deep shadow.

Idly, for her mind was too full for ordered thought, Rosanthe looked at the book which she was still holding: it was bound in firm boards, but covered with a rather fluffy leather, like suede. In the centre of the front cover was a deeply engraven cross resembling the groove in a jewel case shaped to receive a particular pendent. Still without any conscious thought, Rosanthe removed the fine gold chain from her neck and taking the little gold cross, which she had worn since she was a child, placed it over the hollowed depression in the book cover, and found that it fitted in exactly.

As she did so the door opened more widely, and Rosamund ushered in a tall man, who was followed by a crowd of people a good deal shorter than himself. Rosanthe put the book on the table, with the cross still resting on the cover, and sat up on the bed, her head resting against the thin partition wall which separated her from Julian, and waited to see what was about to happen.

And as she did so, she rubbed her eyes, and rubbed again: but the mist was in the room itself, a golden mist swirling round the walls and blotting out all but the circle of light immediately surrounding her. Rosamund was now only a dim figure in the mist, scarcely distinguishable from the tall man who had just come into the room: his companions had vanished entirely—indeed Rosanthe felt uncertain whether she had ever seen them at all—but for a moment she seemed to be aware of a third tall figure very much farther away than either of them.

But before she could begin to wonder who this might be, Rosamund came towards her leading the tall man by the arm, the golden mist fading and running from them like a spent sea foam on low rocks.

"This is my friend Phileros," said Rosamund, "I want you to meet him, Rosanthe; he's just your type, and knows all the right people."

"Delighted, darling, delighted!" Phileros spoke rather languidly, but his handshake was strong. He was smartly dressed, with a touch of the precious about his velvet waistcoat, drooping bow tie and glossy black curls. "Mention my name—sure pass in theatrical circles—all on my watch-chain, Bill, Binkey and the whole crowd—Larry too. Look Rosa, what about something to drink? It's thirsty work getting up a show—nearly as bad as talking to a Duchess!"

Rosamund had the glasses ready, and Rosanthe coughed a little over the unexpected strength of the brew in hers. She had a certain difficulty with her articulation as she spoke:

"You are a producer yourself, then?" she asked.

"In a manner of speaking", said Phileros, waving airy fingers and seating himself beside her on the bed. "Sunday shows, you know; very select; members only; no truck with the Lord Chamberlain—but all the best people. My last was a positive constellation, I can tell you. . . . Look, if you'd care for a part some day, it might be managed," he slipped his arm round her waist as he spoke; "I'm getting a company together at this moment. . . . New play, no license possible—it's based on *Forever Amber* with additions—but stunning cast. . . ."

"I should like it very much; you're very kind," Rosanthe's precise 'enunciation rivalled Eliza Doolittle's, but Phileros did not appear to notice. She drooped her head on to his shoulder—not with any conscious intent, but because her head seemed suddenly too heavy to hold upright; there was a singing buzz in her brain, a tremulous lethargy creeping over her.

"Yes," went on Phileros, as if in thought, "there's a part just made for you. Of course, I'd have to let Pam down. . . . Ann was after it too, and she's quite a draw now. . . . But we might do something about it. . . . I like you, Rosanthe, and you'd be new. . . . I believe in the personal touch—particularly between actress and producer. . . ."

The insinuating purr in his voice should have warned Rosanthe, but her brain was too clouded and sluggish with drink. In another moment Phileros's lips were on her own and she was crushed back against the pillows, his hands moving over her like the tentacles of an octopus. But she had still strength to push him away, and she sat up rigidly as he drew back.

"How dare you?" she began, breathing thickly.

"Oh come, come, darling," drawled Phileros, lighting a cigarette, "all contracts are sealed with a kiss! However, I'm not offended. . . . Your line's a good line, and I respect it—up to a point! But look here, we're forgetting the show! Rosamund darling, go and wake up the Electrics, or something—go and call the quarter anyhow—and kill the amber for God's sake, it gets my goat."

They went into the mist, where, standing at each

side of the room, Rosanthe could see them raising and lowering their arms in a slow rhythm.

She sat back against the wall, her mind a dim turmoil of conflicting thoughts. Rosamund and Phileros seemed to be speaking there; they drew her as their hands beckoned and invited in the mist before her. . . . But she saw the third shadowy figure very far away with still, raised arms; the silence in the room passed into distant music as of a quiet organ heard afar in a very great cathedral, and the music faded into a voice speaking in the clear rich rhythm of correctly spoken verse:

We who have seen the vision of the Quest
Are set apart for pain; but pain is blest
That is endured for the true gift of life—
The knowledge of love through all the years of strife. . . .
 Our thoughts dwell in the kindly lighted hall,
The Garden of the Rose, or, if you would,
Bright Elfland circled round with slain-men's blood,
Circled at least with darkness. . . . Vile shapes crawl
And drape around the windows; and without
Lie the bleak moors, the lonely hills, where call
The plaintive voices of lost things. Evil walks
Abroad upon the fens: with flaming eyes
Comes Grendel to work scathe upon mankind
And drag our souls to dark caves of the mere.
There, pale and bloodless, the long arms of Glam
Wait to entwine our bodies. . . . Dragons there
Lie vigilant above the shining gold,
The glimmer of wealth which is the seeker's bane;
And round the rocks in many a snaky fold
The chill Remora in whose touch lies pain
And frozen terror. . . . There pale vampires drain
The thinning blood—white maidens who draw men

Into their chill cold arms. . . . Morgana sings
In the lonely tower of witchcraft, by the glen
Where monsters lurk; Mathilda weaves her arms
Round mad Ambrosio—all Medeia's charms
Are not more potent than her Lilith-wiles
Which draw him to perdition. Do not stray
Too far away from light: the Snake beguiles
Eve in each heart to pluck the forbidden spray.

The voice passed once more into music, which
faded as the third figure drew backwards through
the mist and disappeared from Rosanthe's sight. But
she was trembling now, and gasping a little as if for
breath; she put her hand to her bosom to still the
beating of her heart, and found that Phileros had torn
away the two pearl buttons which held together the
breast of her blouse. She took the brooch from the
lapel of her jacket and pinned the silk together: it
was a large brooch of shining metal, shaped like a
Grecian lyre, which Julian had given her; and he had
told her more than once how he bought it from an
ancient chapman whom he had met on the road
through the Pleistos valley near Delphi: she seemed
to hear Julian repeating the story: "It was all en-
crusted with dirt—it didn't seem worth a hundred
drachmai really. But I climbed up to the Fountain of
Kastalia and washed it there . . . the spring of the
Muses, the cold clear water from Parnassus the
mountain of song. . . . I did not know why I bought
it, nor why I kept it: but I know now. . . ." Rosanthe
sighed, and then she shook herself suddenly and put
all thoughts of Julian away, for Rosamund was
speaking to her from the edge of the golden mist:

"Rosanthe! Rosanthe! Cut all that out, and attend:
the show is just about to start. I must take part in it,

and you also shall before long. Phileros, you're on the book—not that anyone will need prompting—so you can sit by Rosanthe and explain things to her. Fill the glasses, you old so-and-so, and then let's get cracking."

She whirled away into the mist, and Phileros came clearly into sight, carrying the gin bottle from which he refilled Rosanthe's glass and seated himself beside her on the bed. He waved his hand towards Rosamund with a brisk: "Righty-oh, darling; take them away!" and the mist went up like stage-curtains, showing a clear space in hard blue light where were grouped a number of performers in strange and grotesque costumes.

Of the pageant which followed Rosanthe could never remember more than an indistinct panorama of moving dancers. The music clashed and brayed in a steadily increasing rhythm; Rosamund in a shimmering full skirt and a mere silk wisp of bodice danced among them in sinuous figures, faster and faster as the swing of sound increased, and the hard steel light threw wild and grotesque shadows on the white ceiling.

Phileros, acting as a kind of chorus, kept up a running commentary to Rosanthe, his voice making a husky, crooning understone to the music: "This is the Pageant of the World: we move in the hard light of reality towards the ultimate knowledge of ourselves; we were begotten by chance on a night when our parents had not taken the proper precautions, and we were born with a hundred hereditary taints. Our childhood was conditioned by uncongenial environments, and the folly or ignorance of those amongst whom we found ourselves planted in us the seeds of many a complex and many an inhibition . . .

We all remember the smell of school corridors,
The Lifebuoy soap and the pink cockroach powder;
The mornings of dull distaste in the cold form rooms,
The bread-and-butter pudding at the midday dinner
  table;
The hush of voices past the Headmaster's study. . . .

Whether Phileros was speaking or the mummers in
the dead light, reciting in monotonous monotone,
Rosanthe could not tell. Only, as the pace grew
faster the words of the *récitatif* came in separate
speeches by different speakers or blocks of speakers:

  Thoughts long dormant at last nascent,
Turmoil in the dreams of the adolescent;
A sudden new interest in my own body,
A deeper curiosity about my sister's body;
The chance word of a boy in the sixth form;
Reading Marie Stopes surreptitiously on a bookstall. . . .

And other, higher voices:

  The inane crushes on the younger mistresses;
The aspirin-bottle of gin smuggled into the dormitory. . . .
The sudden change from girl into woman,
The frightened curiosity of new life beginning;
The kiss at the dance, the embrace on the dark staircase;
Or love as a dream, marriage an anathema. . . .

Then the voices of men and women were mingled together so that Rosanthe could only hear odd words or
snatches of sentences as the dance grew faster and
more furious: "Let me kiss you. . . . I'm frightened.
. . . Nothing to fear. . . . Another drink. . . . No one
will know. . . . The door's locked. . . . Locked. . . .
Locked. . . . Don't you want to? . . . It's only natural.

. . . Be realistic. . . . Be modern. . . . Don't be Victorian. . . . You'll grow up if you do. . . . You'll act better if you do. . . . What else is life worth? . . . What else is life for? . . . Everyone does. . . . No one will know. . . . No. . . . Yes. . . . No. . . . Yes. . . . Yes. . . . Yes!" The music in wild turmoil drowning the words and then sinking again as the voices come through once more. "Did you go to the party? . . . My dear, she was stinkin'. . . . Who did you say? . . . With him. . . . How absurd. . . . They gave me a lead. . . . Well, I knew the producer. . . . I went to the races. . . . I went to the hunt ball. . . . He likes them slimmer. . . . He prefers blondes. . . . Come to the party, dance with us, dance with us. . . . Have a good time. . . . You're only young once. . . . Once. . . . Once. . . . Yes, but don't marry him. . . . Only fools marry. . . . Divorce is so easy now. . . . Don't look forward. . . . No marriage is happy. . . . Children are crippling. . . . No more good times. . . . Join in the pageant; come dance with us, dance with us. . . . Drink with us. . . . Laugh with us. . . . Dance with us now. . . . After the dance. . . . Happy, hilarious . . . . After the dance. . . . Romance at the Night-Club. . . . Happiness is change. . . . Responsibility is death. . . . You may die any day. . . . Enjoy yourself now . . . now . . . now . . . Meet interesting people. . . . Travel. . . . Make love. . . . Be made love to. . . . Do everything once, and again if you like it. . . . You like it. . . . We like it. . . . Everyone likes it. . . . Everyone does it. . . . Every sensible person. . . . Be sensible. . . . Be adult. . . . Be modern. . . . Be one of us. . . . one of us. . . . All of us. . . . One of us. . . . One of us. . . ."

Was it the rhythm or the words? Was it the pageant before her or the desires within her? Rosanthe did not know: she had no will to think. But the bright throng was drawing her; she had risen from the bed and moved slowly towards them. The nearer she came, the more she wished to be one of them . . . she could see them clearly now; young men and women, laughing with happiness, chatting brilliantly —she must be one of them at all costs. . . . Then she was among them, whirling in the dance, her hand held by Phileros. . . . She was through them now, and as she turned they came between her and the light of the candles. Then such a fear came upon Rosanthe that all she had known before of terror was a child's dream in the sunlight. For she could see them now as they were, hideous and misshapen, gnarled and twisted; goblins or demons, she could not tell. . . . Surely Rosamund was the incarnate death from *The Ancient Mariner*; and Phileros, what was he with his flabby cheeks and dribbling lips?

She screamed: she broke through them; she reached the end of the bed; she saw the cross resting on the book and strove to reach it. But hands were on her, hard little hands, and great spongy hands, dragging her away. In vain she gripped the bedclothes, they came so easily away in her grasp. Then she cried aloud once: "Julian! Julian! Help me! Oh, Julian!" and the black, weltering tide of unconsciousness broke over her like a great wave filled with evil, gibbering faces—and she remembered no more.

Astrid's Philosophy

So beautiful, she seemed
Almost a living soul. But every part
Was what I made it—all that I had dreamed—
No more, no less: the mirror of my heart,
Such things as boyhood feigns beneath the smart
Of solitude and spring. I was deceived
Almost. In that first moment I believed.

Dymer: C. S. LEWIS.

Julian's mind was in a whirl: the events of the last few hours had not been conducive to clear thinking, and this sudden turn of events was numbing and unnerving. He should have risen to an occasion like this: how often had he dreamed of a sudden emergency in which Rosanthe should be rescued by his resolution, courage and resource! But now he could only stand in the doorway of her room, looking in bewilderment and despair at the disorder of the bed, an overset chair, broken wine glasses.

By degrees his mind began to function again, though still in a slow, turgid way. . . . The open door . . . the window curtains undisturbed . . . no place of hiding in the room. . . . If Rosanthe had been abducted by some person or persons, they surely came and went by the door. . . . He turned and stumbled out into the passage. All was darkness, but he fetched the three-branched candlestick from his bedroom, and made his way slowly in the direction of the open landing above the great staircase.

The white faces of the portraits glimmered past him, seeming to smile or frown as the shadows caught them; the Randle, Urian and Henry, Hawys, Idonea or Isabella of the Middle Ages gave place to the Owen and Meredith and Gryffydd, the Angarhed, Eisylht and Nest of pre-Conquest days, moving faster and faster out of the shadows, through the light and into the forgotten darkness as his speed increased. They seemed like an endless pageant of ghostly figures flitting past him in a nightmare, walling him in from any escape.

When Julian came out at length between the curved portraits of Owen and Angarhed and paused in the big room above the staircase, the fear of that long, long corridor and the endless procession of white, mocking faces was strong on him, so that he set the candlestick on a convenient table and leaned over the back of a tall chair, half gasping, half sobbing, his hands clasping and unclasping round the carved knobs at the corners.

It took him some time to recover his composure; but when he could look about him again, he found himself at a complete loss how to proceed. Opposite him was the dark cavern of the staircase where it descended into the great front hall, whence now came not the faintest glimmer of light, and beyond the turned banisters, which flanked either side of the staircase from the wall to where the first step descended out of the level floor, two passages led away on the upper storey, apparently running parallel, down the length of the house towards the angle whence the short wing jutted to the left.

Despairing of any indication which way to go, Julian shouted as loud as he could: "Rosanthe! Rosanthe!"

But only a distant, mocking echo—"Anthe! Anthe! The! The!" answered him, though he called again and again, standing at the top of the staircase, or at the entrance to one passage or the other.

At length, overcome even more by the strange numbness of will-power, the inability to make any decision, Julian flung himself despondently into the tall chair, and put his face in his hands, striving through a cold, growing panic of despair to think more clearly.

He was roused by the cold, unemotional voice as of water dripping into the pool of unstirred stars, and looking up found Astrid standing at a little distance from him, a black gown thrown over her white dress and a brightly burning lamp of classical pattern held aloft in her right hand.

"Julian," she said, the quiet repose of her voice bringing him immediate peace, "Julian, come with me. You have lost your way; you have lost all sense of the values of this world, all knowledge of the world to come. Follow me, and I will bring you into the quiet cloisters of tranquillity where, all passion spent, the lost shall be found."

Julian rose slowly to his feet: "The lost shall be found," he murmured, already answering to the influence of her thought. "All lost things found . . . Rosanthe. . . . Lost youth, lost dreams, lost stars of my heart; the peace of the early days; the forgetting of the world beyond my heart. And in that escape, a nearer approach to Heaven, nearer even as the earth and the things of this world are banished and left behind. . . . Yes, Astrid, I will follow you, for here all is bitterness and confusion."

As Julian rose, Astrid took him by the hand and led him quickly across the room and into the left-hand passage. He followed her submissively, for the power to make his own decisions seemed to have gone from him absolutely, and she guided him down a narrow way, with many corners, many isolated steps and ramps, until, when all sense of direction was lost to him, they came out suddenly into a large, well-appointed room, furnished as a library, the bookcases round all the walls protected by lattices of gilt wire.

The smell of old books brought Julian still more under Astrid's sway: he was taken back in thought to the early years when his chief pleasure had been to examine and catalogue the neglected eighteenth-century books in his old country home; to long golden afternoons of summer spent in the peace and cool-ness of a College Library which had been a haven from the world since Chaucer read there. The thought of Rosanthe was almost lost to him now as he seated himself mechanically at a table in the centre of the room and began turning over the leaves of a great book which lay open there.

"Here you may remain," said Astrid, "here with books for your truest companions. You and I shall seek together for the secrets of the ancient lore; with Bocthius we shall find the consolations of philosophy; with Agrippa the secrets of the occult; Paracelsus shall show us the true gold; and above all, with Gregory and with Augustine, with Epiphanius and with Aquinas, we shall come, through prayer and fasting, through the denial and abjuration of the world, to the Kingdom of God opening beyond the monastery's tomb. What peace shall be ours in this hermitage of dreams, far from the vulgar bustle of a wicked world! What joy in the knowledge that we alone are wise, alone have found the secret of the true life which shall raise us above mere mankind."

More than ever Julian seemed to be in his old College Library; the aura of rest was all about him, the silence and the quiet light, the feeling of escape from overwhelming responsibilities, choices, conflicting emotions; he seemed to be looking out of one of the narrow, Gothic windows on to the brilliantly sunlit lawn which was crowded with people—living people, shouting, brawling, singing—young men and women talking, arguing, making love; women weeping, men with the shadow of gnawing unhappiness souring their faces: life and death, pleasure and pain laid out before him, all to be striven for, all to be endured, much, perhaps all, to be lost, shredded away like the flesh from a skeleton.

"No, no!" Julian in his mind seemed to be closing the heavily leaded window with trembling fingers; he heard the sudden suppression of the unbearable voices, felt silence fall like a fleecy cloak, saw the sunlight slanting in dim tranquil lines of separate colour through the closed window—and woke with a little shiver to find Astrid bending over his shoulder and pointing out words in the great book which was open before him.

He could not remember afterwards what the book was, nor what he read therein; only, as he read, a great gladness came upon him, a towering spiritual pride that the wise men of old time—yes, and wise men of the present day also, or so it seemed—had thought and written of truths which he himself had found, of conclusions to which at times he himself had come. He did not remember how those shallow sophistries and cowardly half-truths, which he had evolved during years of selfish introspection and a fear-haunted longing for escape, had grown thin and unreal, had been quietly shelved, forgotten or disproved during the last few months since he had known and grown to love Rosanthe. At Astrid's words, and flattered by the concurrence of cunningly selected authorities, he returned to a state of false calm, of a happiness which had worn thin with the years, had grown more and more a resignation filming lightly over the unimagined gulfs of a soul's despair. Once again he sought a God of the dead, to be placated with fasting and with the envious violence of the faster towards those who fast not; once again he followed where the ascetic fallacy led him, into cold cloisters and frustrate hermitages, into life perverted in purging life, into the specious excuses of the paltry sinner gloating over his triumphant conquest of mighty imagined sins which he had never been tempted to commit—Peeping Tom boasting because he was not a Tarquin.

"What of Rosanthe?" a voice seemed to ask him in a moment of light between the shadows—Astrid's voice perhaps, or the voice of that third figure in the mist whose face he had not seen.

"Forget Rosanthe!" it was certainly Astrid's voice speaking to him now. "What comfort can Rosanthe bring? How can you win to the clear light of Heaven with such as she hung as a millstone round your neck? No, rather renounce the way of the flesh— follow the way of the spirit: be the wonder and admiration of all lesser men, you the hermit who will become a saint."

But the distant voice broke in: "A hermit—yes, the hermit of lost dreams! What of the Star of Love that you have followed so long and sought to find, believing that in perfect love true blessedness could be found?"

"How could Rosanthe be your perfect bride of dreams?" Astrid continued. "Even in your love the vile desires of the body predominate—and how do you know that what she feels for you is anything beyond desire?"

"Yes, yes," Julian clutched at the excuse. "Down to the girdle do the gods inherit, below is all the fiend's! I know . . . that accounts. . . . How could I find true spiritual happiness with her? She has brought me so much pain already, so much uneasiness, so wild an awakening of unsatisfied passions. . . . For a little while she loved me—was attracted to me—and now she has changed her mind . . . I *will* forget her; I *will* tear away all that side of myself. Surely it is more blessed so to do? Surely thus I shall draw nearer to the Great Exemplar? Christ did not marry when He was a Man, is not that proof absolute that to forswear the world is the way of righteousness?"

"Yes, yes, proof absolute," Astrid took up his words; "the saints and the philosophers have said it also: read in the book. . . . The Book of Life is to forswear Life, for Death alone is the gateway of Life."

Julian was leaning forward at the table, gripping the edges of the great volume with both hands: "I will forswear the world," he muttered, "I will forget Rosanthe: Astrid, true Star Maiden of pure knowledge, witness my oath. . . ."

He bent forward slowly as if to kiss the book, but as he drew near, his eyes wandered away beyond it and rested upon the picture which was let into the woodwork above the square Jacobean fireplace. It was painted in a great harmony of green, a mighty

garden of trees and a grass-glade shining with daisies
and anemones; otherwise, the only colour was in the
garments of the three figures who were met in the
glade: a naked man wearing only a great cloak of
glowing red flung back from his shoulders; a naked
woman in a cloak of the purest blue who knelt to
one side of him; on the other side another naked
woman, clothed only in the wild abundance of her
flowing hair, concealing and attracting by conceal-
ment, holding and fascinating the eye with calculated
sensuality of pose, of glance, of gesture. It was in
many styles: Morris might have painted the foliage,
only Rossetti could have done justice to the temp-
tress—but who, Julian wondered, could have painted
the Man or the Woman?

As he gazed fascinated, the picture seemed to
shine with a life of its own; the figures seemed to be
moving, the faces turned more direct towards him.
It was "The Choice of Adam," he realised—for
there was no mistaking Lilith of the flaming hair—
but who was Adam? Surely it was in some subtle
way the likeness of himself? . . . And Eve? She was
naked too, more naked than Lilith, but her body
shone for him with a sudden wonder that filled him
with reverence, with a new harmony of feelings. . . .
And then voices spoke, neither in the picture nor in
his mind, yet beyond the range of his vision which
was held by the face of Eve:

Astrid, I love you. All my soul is bent
To worship at your feet, and life is pent
In my heart—life surging to be lived in you,
One with you ever more. . . . Dim knowledge grew
About me even now: I have not lost
One star of all my dreams, nor am I toss'd
Upon the seas of my own evil heart,

For all my soul is yours. . . . Yet life has part
In the most perfect and the holiest love. . . .
Astrid, more beautiful before mine eyes
That dawn's bright angel to the sleeping world
In Eden, when upon a morn of Spring
Adam awoke from sleep to find Eve bending
Among the flower-decked grass, with arms outspread
To welcome him before the birth of sin. . . .
   Oh, we who love are even as pure as they,
Astrid . . . my Eve. . . . Kisses do not betray
In Eden. . . . Let me raise Love's sacrament
To my lips in your own. . . .

The voice—his voice surely, though he did not speak—trailed away into a sob as of unutterable yearning, and Astrid answered, speaking in strong, cold tones as if some power spoke through her with more than mortal finality:

       The night is rent
With bitter daylight; and dreams cannot live
Past the cold morning. In them we but give
Life's picture a false being drawn from ours,
A soulless Galatea; blind fancy dowers
The idol we have made with our own hope,
Our easy answers to unanswered life,
Striving to fill the night wherein we grope
With an imagined sun that conquers strife
And makes all plain. . . . For, Julian, you have made
Me in this likeness—you who are afraid
Of your own heart, who do not dare to meet
Life as it is, but seek, for dreams are sweet,
To hide from truth behind truth's own bright veil,
And fade, soul-emptied, into a breathing tomb.
In me there is no life—a shadow, pale

And unsubstantial as the silent moon
Casts on the sleeping earth. What you would seek
In wilful blindness you will surely find:
Nor must you blame me if I seem to wreak
A heartless vengeance on you. Being blind
By your own choice, hiding your eyes from pain,
Shunning endeavour, holding life a vain
And wicked garment of weeds, you must not deem
That you have been betrayed. For you blaspheme
Against the very Love which is your Quest,
Holding your Maker made you so amiss
That His good gifts, used rightly, should defile.
You cannot tread the earth as a man treads
Yet live, as might a spirit, upon air:
It is the fear and not the deed is vile;
The coward who forswears what he most dreads—
The man accepts what other men must dare.

When Astrid finished speaking, the spell which held Julian seemed to be broken, and he sprang to his feet, turning with raised arm as if to strike her.

But he paused when he saw her: for now Astrid clung to the edge of the table, marble white and trembling like a leaf.

"Do not cast me off!" she moaned, "I led you so near to the truth: it was only the garments of your heart that disguised me, the star-spun robes with which you clothed me in despite of reason. . . ."

Her voice quavered into silence, and out of the silence grew a murmur as of a great wind waking among trees; swiftly it grew in volume, loud as the thunder of waves on the Cornish coast, deep as the roar of seas beneath the imprisoning ice. But through it for a moment came the music which Julian had heard before, and the voice of Rosanthe singing:

Here in the heart for ever dwelling,
　　Lost in the heart that seeks me there;
Flesh of your flesh by flesh compelling,
　　Still must Ixion clasp the air.

The song was lost in the roar of the wind: the casements broke open with a crash of shivering glass, and a great gust tore screaming through the room, whirling away Astrid like a leaf before it, scattering books and papers over the floor, putting out all the lights so that in a moment Julian was in complete darkness.

The gust passed into absolute silence, and Julian, breathing hard, groped his way to the door, and went stumbling along the uneven passage towards the open landing at the head of the staircase.

"How could I have wasted so many precious minutes?" he muttered. "God grant I am not too late. . . . Oh, Rosanthe, Rosanthe my darling. . . ."

The Bower and the Book

She gathered up her glittering hair,
And round his neck its tresses threw,
And twined her arms of beauty rare
Around him . . . and cried the while: . . .
   "These lips are mine; the spells have won them,
Which round and round thy soul I twine;
And be the kiss I print upon them
Poison. . . ."

        Rhododaphne: THOMAS LOVE PEACOCK.

Stumbling and striking himself against walls and wainscots as the passage turned, Julian groped his way until he came to the open room whence Astrid had led him.

Here, to his surprise, all was light, with many candles burning in sconces on the walls, and a lamp set on the table above the dark chasm of the stairs. A figure was bending over the table, turning the pages of a book; as Julian stumbled into the room she looked up, and he saw that it was Rhoda, dressed now in a long red gown or "house-coat" coming almost to her feet.

"You're looking for Rosanthe," she said as soon

as she saw him. "I was waiting here to help you find her. Wherever have you been?"

"With Astrid," answered Julian almost with a groan. "She persuaded me to accompany her to the library, and there stuffed me full of cheap philosophies and specious arguments for shirking the responsibilities of life, until I very nearly forgot Rosanthe and forswore the world."

"I was afraid she might have done that," Rhoda said, pursing her lips and shaking her head wisely until the long curls swirled and gleamed in the candle-light like a halo. "You were always rather inclined to believe in her kind of nonsense. . . . Look, Julian: do get all this ascetic tripe out of your head. Oh, I know you believe in the Good Life and in the Divine Example, and all that; well, why not? Hundreds of men do—and quite a number of women also. But that's no reason to run away from every day; you say you want to live in To-morrow, but ninety-nine times out of a hundred you succeed only in living in some idealised yesterday—which is sheer escapism, and blasphemous at that. Come now, you've got enough sense to see that there is no real escape, not at least without accompanying damnation. After all, your religion tells you that God made man and woman and told them to live together in the normal way—to be a mutual comfort and help to one another, as well as merely to continue the species."

"Yes, I'm sure you're right," agreed Julian hesitating in front of her, "but look, Rhoda: I can't stop to argue now, I must find Rosanthe."

"Of course," Rhoda hastened, "and she must have gone down the other passage. (The lower floor is quite out of the question—all dark and unknown.) Come along with me. My room is at the end of the passage, and you'd better rest there for a little while and have something to eat and drink: you look about done in, and you'll only collapse if you don't give yourself a chance. Here, take my arm."

Julian certainly felt strangely sick and giddy, and he gladly availed himself of the arm which Rhoda held out to him. She took the lamp in her other hand, and together they set forth along the right-hand passage in which there were no corners, although it curved a little to the left.

"As I was saying," Rhoda resumed, "it's blasphemous, and damned cowardly, to condemn all the physical side of life in the way Astrid does. And that sort of thing breeds its own nemesis, too, in the shape of repressions, inhibitions and the like; all goes smoothly for some time, and then everything breaks down, and you're lucky if the reaction comes simply in a normal direction. More often than not it takes the form of some frightful aberration, and then you're a hundred times nearer damnation than if you had just taken the world as you found it, and had a good time in a natural way when you got the chance."

"Oh, I agree," said Julian earnestly. "But virtue and . . . and continence, and so on, isn't really a forswearing—it's only a regulation: man the spirit in control of man the animal, and not vice-versa. One of the greatest virtues has always been moderation: even the early Greek philosophers agreed on that."

"Yes, moderation is a very fine thing," said Rhoda. "But that also can so easily be abused; it should never become an end in itself, for example; it should always be used as part of a greater purpose. To me moderation is the apéritif to excess. And the Greeks agreed with me, too: didn't they follow a year of lawful and sedate living by the wild license of the festivals, the pornographic comedies, the drunken revels in honour of Dionysos, and the complete absence of everyday morality during the nocturnal orgies of the Tauropolia? Wise people, the Greeks; purge the emotions from time to time; don't be afraid to admit that you have emotions—after all, everyone has them, in greater or less degree; call a spade a spade, and remember that Adam was the first gardener."

So Rhoda talked on, her mouth very close to Julian's ear, her hair brushing his cheek, his arm pressed closely into her side.

As he grew drowsy at her voice, lethargic in determination, inability to control his thoughts came over him. And, as if in answer to quiet, insistent promptings from within, he began to notice the pictures on the walls of the passage: at first the subjects were simply mythological, but by degrees they began to take on a more immediate and personal meaning for him, growing more exciting to the senses even as the senses grew more excited. The subject did not change, only the method of presenting them: Danae and the Shower of Gold; Pasiphae and the Bull; Hephaistos and Athena; Herakles and Auge; Dionysos and Nikaia; Zeus and Alkmena—all presented with a wealth of detail and a warmth of colour, but more subtle in suggestion, more calculatedly sensual in appeal as they went along.

By the time they reached the end of the passage and came down two steps, between heavy curtains, and into Rhoda's room, Julian's head was resting on her shoulder, and his arm was about her waist. Once more he was walking as if in a dream, but the blood pulsed loudly through his veins, dimming his eyes, while the beating of his heart seemed ready to choke him.

The room was small and shadowy; stiflingly warm, and heavy with the perfume of incense. It was lit by a tall, flaming brazier of aromatic woods, and Rhoda extinguished her lamp as soon as they came within the curtains.

"Sit down and rest," she said, leading Julian to a couch which was set immediately beside the tall tripod of the brazier. She did not withdraw from his arm, however, but sat for a little while beside him before taking up a full glass of red wine from a low table and handing it to him. She took another herself, and bade him drink.

Julian raised the glass to her—and for a moment the fear came on him again, for through the wine he could see Rhoda's face horribly distorted into the likeness of the face of iron upon the door of the House of Fear. But the fire which throbbed within him forbade him to take warning, and with a cry that was half terror, half bravado, he set the glass to his lips and drained it at a draught, letting it fall and shatter on the floor.

Then madness came upon Julian as the wine coursed like Grecian fire through his veins. A red, stifling mist closed in and swirled above him, in which he could see Rhoda and Rhoda alone, shining white between the glowing red waves of her gown. She was singing to him now in a low, sibilant voice like dry honey dripping into the sunlight, and the sound of it and the thick-coming fancies choking into his brain like over-sweet wood-smoke set every limb trembling and his lips twitching. He could not hear the words of the song; he did not wait for it to finish, but with a stifled cry he turned upon Rhoda, crushing her back across the bed and leaning over her like a beast of prey.

White she glimmered through the red mist, her eyes clouded with desire, her lips rising to meet his. With a cry that had little of the human in it he flung himself upon her—and in the brief moment which parted her body from his, he lived a life longer than an age in Hell.

It was Rhoda to whom he was drawing so near; and then it was Rhoda no longer, but Rosanthe— Rosanthe with a terror beyond death in her eyes, Rosanthe screaming and struggling to escape from the beast that had been Julian. He screamed too, with the fingers of angels tearing at his heart—and it was Rhoda again, but Rhoda dead, ghastly—with empty, staring eyes and white, cold body; and as he fell towards her, she decayed away, until he held in his arms a dry, bleached skeleton, which, even as he touched it, crumbled into a little heap of fine, white dust.

And in that unnamed terror of agony and loathing Julian's senses forsook him.

Yet the singing darkness and the great fall into bottomless space did not bring complete oblivion. He was moving in the darkness, and shapes moved about him; but he saw them through shut eyelids like forms passing between him and a very bright light. He heard winds moaning, seas muttering, thunder growling, hills falling; he went on through an endless labyrinth of unseen obstacles, groping, groping towards an unknown resting-place.

But at length the noises faded and a sense of repose seemed to wipe out all recollection of the horror that he had known; there came the glorious peace of a sudden ending to pain; a tranquillity as of the laying down of an over-cruel spiritual burden. The noises were a distant hum like the indistinguishable murmur of bird and bee over quiet gardens on a summer's evening; the murmur grew into music, the music into Rosanthe's voice singing:

Here in the world to eyes scarce seeing
Hid and revealed in your desire,
Ghost of the peace that still is fleeing
Eternal fledgeling of the fire.

The voice died into peace, and Julian opened his
eyes. For a little while he did not know where he was,
nor could he remember more than a dim shadow of
his recent experiences. He was kneeling beside a bed
in a great quiet room, and he thought at first that it
was his own room and that he had fallen asleep
while saying his prayers. But as he sat back on his
heels and looked about him, he realised that he was
once more in that room deep in Eclwyseg Manor—
or in the House of Fear—where Rosanthe had slept,
and which he had found empty when he came in
answer to her cry for help.

Still kneeling, he began to arrange and assemble
his thoughts: the corridor, the room above the stairs,
Astrid . . . Rhoda. . . . Then he remembered, but
without any curiosity, scarcely with any horror or
remorse. These had been the follies of adolescence:
now suddenly he knew that he was a man.

He thought of Rosanthe, and realised dimly that
she too had changed for him, though in what way he
could not tell. Only there was no longer any conflict
in his thoughts of her: she was the woman whom he
loved; she was the friend for whom no sacrifice was
too great; she was something more than either, more
subtly personal, more infinitely universal—more than
a symbol of the Divine Thought, less only than the
incarnation of the Divine Word.

As Julian knelt by the bed, a glimmer of gold
caught his eye on the table; stretching out his hand
he reached down the leather-bound book on the
cover of which Rosanthe's little golden cross still lay

enshrined. He lifted it out with reverent fingers, set the long, fine chain about his own neck, kissed the cross since it was hers, and slipped it into the front of his own shirt. Still kneeling, and holding the book in his hands, he opened at random and turned the pages without noticing the contents until suddenly it fell open as at an accustomed place and the words seemed to surge up towards him: "Oh God, from Whom all holy desires, all just thoughts do proceed, Whose service is perfect freedom, give unto Thy servants that peace which the world cannot give. . . ."

For a moment the words brought only memories and associations: the little Saxon church at home, the quiet, kind voice of the old Rector who had prepared him for Confirmation; the flickering candlelight in the vast empty spaces of the College chapel attended perfunctorily from time to time; hurrying through the evening service at the University church as merely the prelude to the sermon by some well-known preacher. . . . But memory and association merged speedily together, became uncomfortable, rather troubling—just as of late the thought of religion, the simple, well-known words of texts and of liturgies had become troubling. Then with a sudden overwhelming light, with a breaking of gates and a flooding in of peace, with an utter reliance and an utter reliability, a supreme surrender and a supreme assumption of responsibility, with an undefinable host of mind-pictures wherein Rosanthe was mingled inextricably and with absolute propriety, there came to Julian the power of prayer; and he, who had knelt so often with hands folded and lips shaped to divine words, prayed now for the first time in his life.

And when he had finished praying, he rose slowly to his feet, replaced the book on the table beside the bed, and stood for a little while considering what he must do next. After a moment's thought, he began to examine the room with deliberate care, sounding the floor and walls for secret doors, and making certain that the window was latched from within.

When his examination was completed, he went to the door and looked out along the passage. There was a light in the distance which he knew must be in the room at the top of the great staircase, but he returned to the bedside and picked up the three-branched candlestick which stood there, experiencing as he did so the strange feeling of repeating an action which he could never remember to have performed.

With only a moment's pause, Julian again passed through the doorway, and walked quickly along the corridor between the lines of portraits until he came again into the open room where the candles still burned in the many sconces round the walls. Opposite him again was the dark well of the staircase, and on either side of it the two passages leading into the unknown depths of the house; and standing, one in the entrance of each passage, were Astrid and Rhoda.

Without pausing, Julian advanced to the head of the staircase and prepared to descend; but as he set his foot on the first tread Astrid called out to him:

"Julian, Julian! Be careful what you are doing! Think before you act! Is this the course of a reasonable human being, of a modern man with a modern grasp of reality? Rosanthe has been carried away into unknown places; can you help her by endangering yourself? Self-preservation is the first Christian duty —for charity begins at home, and self-destruction is the blackest of sins. So wait: look before you leap; consider whether after so much time wasted there is any real possibility of finding Rosanthe at all; and if there is no chance, be philosophic, be resigned; it's no use crying over spilt milk!"

Julian had hesitated when Astrid began to speak, but now he was moved only to laughter by the trite hollowness of her reasoning.

"Go back to school, Lady Astrid," he said, "learn a fresh stock of empty platitudes; they cannot influence me now."

"But Julian, think!" cried Astrid desperately— "Are all the dreams of so many years, the aspirations, the conclusions of all your lonely thoughts— are these all to be cast away together because, forsooth, you think you have discovered a way to gain the world as well as to save your own soul?"

"Had I followed you still," retorted Julian, "I should have lost my own soul as well as losing the world."

"Ah, Julian, you will lose the world indeed!" it was Rhoda who spoke now as she leaned indolently over the carved banisters above him, the dark oak drawing the gauzy thinness of her blouse tightly about the curves of her figure. "You think that you can be man and spirit at once; but consider, you poor romantic fool: you say that you love Rosanthe, all well and good; for her and for her sake, you will seek purity—you will remain a virgin (what a word to apply to a man!) until you lose it to her alone. Poor Julian! How many men will she have slept with by the time your turn arrives? And even if she too remains chaste, supposing you should lose her at the last, or she should turn you down: oh, Julian, what you will have missed never to have held a woman in your arms, never to have . . ."

"Stop it, you bloody little bitch!" broke in Julian, with more vehemence than he intended. "The risk's worth taking, if you must look at it like that. And anyhow, sex isn't the only thing in life—any more than it's the only thing in love—or in marriage. But I don't believe that I shall lose her: certainly I shall lose nothing of any importance by loving her—indeed I shall gain, I have already begun to gain, more, far more than you could even begin to understand, or I to explain—yes, though I never so much as kiss her on the lips. And if you think that your nasty, prurient, sixth-form aids to beastliness, your cheap, gutter-flaunting, seventh-veil attempts at seduction are going to have any serious effect on the straight-forward, honest love of an ordinary man for an ordinary woman—well you'd better go back to night-school until your mental development catches up with your physical!"

Julian paused, grimly amused at his sudden gift for abusive epithet, but Rhoda only laughed mockingly:

"You'll ride that new hobby-horse of yours to death before long," she jeered. "You'll get tired of it soon enough. Just wait until the right time comes: a good meal, a few dirty stories, a drink or two more than is wise for you—you won't say 'no' to me then, my fine, flaunting satyr masquerading as a Dresden-china shepherd—and you'll think of enough specious excuses too! Never mind, Julian, I can bide my time; you can never escape far from me, and I am always waiting when least expected. . . . Now look: experience is a deuced good thing: just imagine the wedding night with Rosanthe if you didn't know how. . . ."

"I've had enough of this!" Julian spoke quietly, but the note of purpose in his voice silenced Rhoda instantly, and she cringed away, her face and figure grown suddenly old and wrinkled.

"You are going to a useless death," murmured

Astrid, "you are throwing away your God-given talents: you were to have been a poet, a great interpreter to man of the Will of God; your name was to have gone down to time . . ." but her voice trailed off into purposeless alliterations of names, "Sophocles, Shakespeare, Sheridan, Shaw; Marlowe, Milton, MacDonald, Morris. . . ."

Julian did not wait to argue, however; without another glance at her or at Rhoda, he set his foot to the second step and began to descend into the darkness. At the twelfth step he came to a square landing of flat uncarpeted wood from which the next flight descended into the hall. Holding the candle aloft he stepped briskly across this space; but before he reached the other side, the whole square tilted steeply behind him, and in a moment he had lost his footing and was shot down a slippery glissade of wood and precipitated into complete darkness underneath the flight of stairs which he had just descended.

Rosanthe Presides

Little men hurrying, running here and there,
Within the dark and stifling walls, dissent
From every sound, and shoulder empty hods:
—"The god's great altar should stand in the crypt
Among our earth's foundations."
Babel: GORDON BOTTOMLEY.

Rosanthe's senses returned to her very slowly, as consciousness comes back after the crisis of a serious illness. At first the sense of touch made itself manifest, and she knew that she was sitting in a straight-backed chair of cold stone, dank to the touch of her hands which rested on carved stone bosses, and cold to her arms which from the elbow lay along the smooth flat arms of the chair. Then she became aware of the smell of the place in which she was: many mingling scents, of earth, of mildew, of stagnant water, of vegetable and even animal decay, and of dead, chill draughts of air which whistled through the place without ever freshening the atmosphere. Sound came next: a confused harsh murmur of voices, throaty laughter, guttural exclamations, high-pitched indignation, and behind all the steady drip of water, dead and distinct through the splash of wine into goblets, the clink of metal upon stone.

With difficulty Rosanthe opened her eyes—and shut them again hastily to keep out the evil dream which would not end. But in a little while, as the sounds still continued, Rosanthe raised her eyelids slowly and looked about her without moving.

What manner of place she was in was not easy to determine, for it was of vast extent and dimly lighted. It was built of stone, low-roofed, supported by innumerable pillars stretching away into the darkness. She was seated in a great stone chair at the head of a table piled high with strange-looking fruits, all of which seemed to be of a white, grey or pale-green colour; and round the table was assembled such a company that she might well believe that she was still dreaming. They seemed to be men and women, but all were below the normal height, many were deformed, all had the same wizened faces and pronounced features, the same unhealthy complexions and sunken, fishy eyes. They were dressed in odd, antiquated costumes, tunics of a mouldy green, belts of faded leather, legs swathed in sacking cross-gartered with rusty red; their hair was unkempt, the men's faces unshaven, though few had full beards, and their teeth glinted yellow between thin, tight lips which appeared always to be grinning weakly. This strange scene was lit by a few flaring, smoking torches stuck into rings in the pillars nearest to the table, casting weird lights and shadows into the surrounding gloom.

She moved a little now, clasping the carved ends of the chair-arms with her fingers as if to test the reality of all about her. At once the tall, slim figure of Rosamund bent down over her left shoulder.

"So you've come to at last," she said. "How silly

to pass out like that just when the dance was working up to a good climax! Never mind; we brought you along down here; there is always a feast, you know—after the dance!"

"You should have left me where I was," said Rosanthe rather shakily. "And who are all these people? I don't think I like to be near them."

"These? Oh, pals of ours. As a matter of fact they all belong to you."

"To me? What do you mean?"

"They're your company now. They elected you principal, a little while ago, while you were unconscious."

"But I don't want to have anything to do with them," protested Rosanthe.

"You can hardly back out now. Think of the fuss. Think of the publicity. Think what a fool you'd feel. Oh, they're harmless, dear creatures; you'll get to love them before long, and then you'll wonder how you ever did without them."

Rosanthe was about to protest again, but just at that moment a commotion broke out round the table.

"You spilt my wine on purpose!" yelled one little man, hurling the empty goblet at another near the farther end of the table—infinitely too far away to have interfered with the first speaker's drinking arrangements.

"He spilt it on purpose!" vociferated half the company.

"It's a bloody lie!" screamed several others.

"Lynch him!" yelled one.

"Put his head in the water butt!" squeaked another.

In a moment pandemonium reigned; fruit and utensils were used as missiles; fists, feet, teeth and nails as weapons. Rosanthe shrank back in her chair appalled, glancing with loathing at the vicious faces and primitive methods of the combatants.

But the battle lasted only a matter of minutes; peace returned with as little prelude as war. The company seemed to forget all animosity, all griev-ances, as they settled down to the interrupted meal, talking and jabbering away once more as if nothing had happened.

"Not an ounce of vice in one of them!" remarked Phileros emerging from behind Rosanthe's chair on the other side. "The only trouble is that they don't know their own minds from one minute to the next; but it adds to the variety of life—and there's nothing nicer than continual change. You'll get used to them in no time! Here, try some of this fruit, it's top-hole!"

He held a silver dish before Rosanthe who chose out a little bunch of white grapes. She bit into one, and found it sour and rather tasteless, but finished those on her plate in a perfunctory manner.

"Well now," said Rosamund, pouring out a goblet of wine for Rosanthe, "I hope you are getting more accustomed to your new subjects? They all worship you, I can tell you! Don't you just worship the Lady Rosanthe?" she asked of the company, and a babel of voices arose:

"Long live Rosanthe! Rosanthe for ever! For she's a jolly good fellow! Queen Rosanthe! The Queen can do no wrong!"

For the first time Rosanthe felt a little glow of affection for her motley followers.

"Speak to them!" suggested Phileros, and the com-pany took up the suggestion:

"Speech! Speech! We want Rosanthe! We want Rosanthe!" She rose slowly to her feet, still support-ing herself by the carved heads on the chair-arms, amid loud applause that speedily died down as her lips began to move:

"My friends," she began, rather nervously, "it gives me much pleasure to—to be among you to-night. It—it's—er, very kind of you to elect me—I mean, I esteem it a very great honour" ("Hear! hear! Long live Rosanthe!" from several of the crowd), "and I shall try—I mean strive—to, to discharge every obligation of my new position." ("Three cheers for Rosanthe!" yelled the company.) "My friends, I must beg you to forgive me the many short-comings of this my first public speech. But I cannot end without once again expressing my . . . my deep appreciation of the honour which you have done me."

She sat down with rather a sensation of having made a fool of herself in public. But the crowd yelled with delight, clapped, banged the table, and cheered, while Phileros remarked:

"Eminently acceptable; pithy, terse and to the point; sure insight into human nature. Really, Rosanthe, I congratulate you! Born orator!"

"I . . . I didn't say anything very much," she ventured, though the glow of approbation raised by Phileros's words really filled her with doubt as to what she actually had said.

"Ah, that was the art of it," purred Phileros, "the simple touch; the profound truth couched in an original and straightforward sentence—that's the only way to reach the heart of the people. The academic search for precise shades of meaning, the pedantic insistence on polysyllables—that's all hooey, no use here. You know, Rosanthe, where you'll end up is in parliament!"

There was no irony in Phileros's tone, and the insidious flattery seemed already to have gone to Rosanthe's head. She leaned back complacently in the chair, sipping her wine, and watching with pleased amusement the odd behaviour of the company at the table. For besides the occasional brawl in which most of them would become involved from time to time, there was many another unexpected feature to divert her. Now one would rise and begin a speech, only to change his mind in the middle of a word, and sit down with it uncompleted; now another would break off in the midst of a story, having lost interest before the point was reached; some would collect great piles of fruit on their plates, taking a bite or two out of each and then going on to the next; others would play complicated games resembling chess, using the half-filled goblets as pieces, but would break off to drink, or suddenly sweep the whole game into their opponent's lap with a movement of the arm.

"You know," Rosamund remarked to her presently, "you've quite won the hearts of them all. As Phileros says, you've a future before you: go in for public life, that's obviously your line. Of course, you'll get beyond this kind of gathering very soon, but it's as well to begin at the beginning. You've exceptional gifts, and, provided you stick to the job and don't get side-tracked by anything—or anyone— you'll get to the top of the tree before you're thirty. But the great thing is clear thinking; regulate your life and cut out the unessential. Enjoy emotion to the full, but never let it get control of you—that's why marriage is so pernicious; you get hitched in a moment of sexual intoxication, and there you are, your whole career finished."

'But Rosamund, dear," ventured Rosanthe, though tentatively and without conviction, "surely one can be married *and* have a career? Julian has always agreed with me over that. He is a writer and archæ-

ologist, and I am to become an actress, if I fail to
get a university lectureship. . . ."

"My dear, you really don't believe in all that sort
of talk, do you?" interrupted Rosamund. "Marriage
is still a full-time job for a woman—certainly now
when you can't get servants. Do you think Julian
would do a hand's turn in the house—once you were
married? Not if I know men! And anyhow, I doubt if
he'll marry you when it comes to the point. He's a
successful writer; he's the greatest living authority on
something or other to do with digging up things in
Greece— Delphian Ceramics, whatever that means—
and he'll be famous pretty soon. Then do you think
you'll be his cup of tea any longer? Not likely! He'll
find some wonderful excuse—facing facts with a
religious basis, as like as not—and marry for rank
or money before the year's end. Oh, he'll find out his
mistake—when it's too late; for you're worth ten of
him, and will make ten times more of a mark in the
world. . . . Jolly good riddance!"

"He's not like that! He's not!" Rosanthe was
troubled, but would not admit it even to herself.
"Julian isn't that kind at all: he doesn't change. . . ."
("Die-hard conservative, in life as in everything
else," interjected Rosamund.) "And I *know* that I
can depend upon him whatever happens. Love
doesn't mean a passing attraction to Julian; it's a life-
long faith with him, and he has pledged it to me.
Oh, I know I laugh at it sometimes—and at other
times I'm frightened at it—but I *do* believe in its
reality."

Phileros whistled long and loud, and Rosamund
broke out:

"Do you really mean to say that you're still taken
in by such romantic nonsense? Well, it's high time
somebody told you the facts of life! Why do you

think your precious Julian hasn't come to your rescue yet? He knows perfectly well where you are, and he has only to come down the stairs into this crypt. But he won't turn up, not Julian, he's far more pleasantly employed. I'm sorry to hurt you, my dear, but at this moment your new Galahad, the pure and saintly Julian, is in bed with my sister Rhoda."

"She's a one," interjected Phileros with feeling. "Knows how to get the most out of life does Rhoda!"

"It's not true! I don't believe it!" cried Rosanthe springing to her feet. "Julian would never even think of such a thing—far less do it. I hate you! I hate you all!" She burst into tears as she sank back into the chair and, leaning forward on the table, buried her face in her hands. And as she shut out the sight of that fantastic company, of the piled table and the torchlight flickering on the squat stone pillars, the tears seemed to wash away even the fire-drawn likeness of the scene which remains with the seer who is plunged suddenly from bright light into darkness. For the first time in a very long period, so it seemed to Rosanthe, she was thinking of someone other than herself; and with the sudden urge to defend Julian came back something of the clearness of mind which she had lost for so long, some perception of the distorted way in which she had been made to look at things.

Rosamund's voice cut through her thoughts as warm lint on an aching wound separates the pain for a little moment:

"Rosanthe dear, he's only human. You are human too. Face facts, my dear: life is only horrible if you try to look at it through the chinks in a shutter of romance. But romance stifles the living air in a room and hedges you into a morbid, frightened twilight where you will grow fretful, ailing, and in the end

pine away. Open the shutters, fling wide the casements, let in the joyous sunlight and the healthy
fresh air. Life was made to live: Julian is living it to
the uttermost at this moment: do likewise—he's not
the only man in the world. . . ."

But Rosamund had made a false move: for
Rosanthe shivered and drew away, hurt in an oddly
deep way by the fact that Rosamund had chosen
to illustrate her text the symbol which Julian had
used to her once, of how love had come to him and
changed all his world. And even as she thought, she
heard Julian's voice speaking to her in the lines
wherein he had afterwards enshrined the thought:

> Oh my beloved, when you came to me—
> Moving like sunlight through a darkened room
> And opening dust-greyed shutters to the day—
> The mimic childhood and the crippled youth
> Fell from me, autumn leaves upon the breeze
> Of next year's March; and as a man I stood
> Upon the sea-damp shingle of my being,
> And knew you what you were. . . .

While the voice spoke, Rosanthe realised that the
continuous noise of voices round the table had
ceased, and that complete silence fell when the words
ceased. A sudden trembling seized her, and as she
opened her eyes and saw Julian standing at the opposite end of the table, she knew that she had known
he was there a moment before she actually perceived
him.

"Julian!" she cried wildly, "that poem—'you know
me what I am'—do you really know me? Do I really
know you?"

And Julian answered, his quiet assured voice coming like a breath of fresh air into an overheated room

after the querulous, staccato tones of the company at the table:

"Rosanthe, no human being can know another to the end of every mood and of every moment, every noble prompting and every vile temptation: such knowledge is the ever-presence of the God who was also a man. . . ."

"Now, boys, for a Scripture Union meeting on Margate sands!" drawled Phileros, but Julian continued as if he had not noticed the interruption.

"But you and I, Rosanthe—and many a thousand others such as you and I—can draw a little nearer to that knowledge, share a little more of the Divine Nature, in the light of that undefined gift which we call love."

"Natural desires dressed up in pantomime properties," Phileros's voice was the acme of condescension. "How tenacious is the Victorian craze for clothing the simple body of reality in hideous and stifling garments from Mrs. Grundy's sewing-room!"

"You who speak so," said Julian as if noticing Phileros for the first time, "are one of those who have never known what love is—and perhaps now can never know. Rosanthe, Rosanthe, do you not see! *Of course* we are human, you and I, and are moved deeply, overwhelmingly by our purely human desires. We are tempted, and we fall—actually, or only in thought—to the wiles of the Rose of Passion, the snares of the Lover of Desire. They stand beside you now; they have stood beside me also; they are never very far from any of us. But their love, the most ancient of all false loves—the love of Lilith, if you like—is a vain and sterile love. Oh, Rosanthe, do you not see? Knowledge is love: love alone can bring knowledge, such knowledge as may grow between you and me; the mutual service of the soul, which is the most perfect freedom; the natural attraction between man and woman which is the holy desire; the understanding and the sacrifice of the mind in which lies the fount of all just thoughts: Love alone can give us that peace which the world cannot give— no passive bed of luxury, no austere ascetic rule, no blindfold centre way of self-sufficiency, but a mountain path of sharp rocks and clinging briars; pain which is the gate of life; care the companion of joy; anxiety the camp-followers of happiness. The many discordant voices of the world will mock us, the many meddling fingers will overset the lights and scatter the banquet; darkness may divide us and crowds may sever us: but love does not perish in the fire, it rises out of pain into newer and more glorious life. The true Rose is not ours to pluck: but when once it has been set upon our hearts—the gift that is not given by choice alone—it shines there for ever, as love receives all love by giving. . . ."

As he spoke, Julian had leaned forward over the end of the table, and Rosanthe had leaned forward too, so that in time they could see only one another at either end of a lane of light and shadow the sides of which were hedged by a darkness full of moving faces, and between them the long stone table with its heaped dishes of fruit and flasks of wine.

But as Julian continued speaking, a murmur arose all about them, a muttering growl of dissent which rose louder and louder, though still Julian's voice rang clear above it, until suddenly wild pandemonium broke in upon them. The company surged together across the table, scattering dishes and their contents in confusion, and all the torches were torn from their sockets and trodden under foot, plunging the whole vault into utter darkness.

Through it all Rosanthe and Julian struggled to

reach one another: "Julian, Julian! Where are you?" she cried, "I've lost you! I can't come to you, I've no sense of direction any longer, and I'm all hemmed in."

And she heard his voice: "Rosanthe, stay where you are! I'm coming to you, but it's slow work getting through this cursed clinging, yelling crowd. Stay where you are, my darling, don't go with them: I shall reach you in time."

But the pressure of the unseen hordes was too much for Rosanthe: for a moment she clung desparingly to the side of the chair, but she felt her fingers slipping over the smooth stone, the tug of the crowd drawing her like the under-wash of the outgoing tide dragging at the legs of a spent swimmer clinging to a rock—and then she was whirled away in the heart of the throng. And though she still cried desperately to Julian, she could hear his answering voice grow fainter and fainter until it was lost in the darkness and turmoil behind her.

Whither she was going she could not tell, nor how long the nightmare rush of unseen struggling figures continued round about her. She had a sense of being led on a zig-zag, haphazard course between and around unseen obstacles; often her hand brushed against a cold, damp wall or pillar, or her foot struck against the square corner of a column's base—on and on for an indeterminable length of time. And then suddenly she saw a faint light ahead, a pale white radiance proceeding from above. Her companions swerved aside, yelling and cursing more loudly than ever, but for the first time she managed to direct her own course, and in a few moments realised with a gasping sense of relief that she was alone.

But she sped on, in terror lest they should return and drag her away. The light ahead grew brighter, more definite as she went; and soon she recognised it for a shaft of moonlight streaming down a long narrow staircase approached by an arched doorway in the wall. Through it she hastened, and sped up the steps, up, up, until she came suddenly out into the cool summer night and found herself in an open, grassy glade of a great, dark wood stretching steeply uphill in front of her.

The Phoenix in the Maze

When through the old oak forest I am gone,
   Let me not wander in a barren dream,
But when I am consumed in the fire,
Give me new Phœnix wings to fly at my desire.
   Sonnet on reading "King Lear": JOHN KEATS.

    Rosanthe wanted to stop and fling herself down in the long grass through sheer delight at having escaped at length from the House of Fear; but still there was the haunting dread of pursuit, the shadow of the Fear yet clutching at her and bringing an occasional sob into her throat. So she sped on, up the long grassy ride between the oak trees, until she came to the end of it where a tall, dark pinewood began.

    Here Rosanthe paused to look about her and to rest for a little while. She had climbed considerably since she came out into the night, and she could see the House beneath her, the gable at its end showing white through the trees. She turned her back on it with a little shiver, and looked to see where she should go next. To the left and ahead the side of the pass closed in more and more steeply, the trees

185

clinging precariously to the hillside until it became
too precipitous to hold any vegetation. On the other
side of the pass rose the even more perpendicular
cliffs of the bastion-like mountain range which swept
up the valley end where she could see the lonely
tower of Dinas Bran on its spur of rock. The bottom
of the pass lay only a little way beneath her on the
right, ascending steeply parallel to the way that
she had come.

Rosanthe looked up the pass and saw the sides
closing in until they hid the impassable head of it:
yet into that lonely and forbidding cul-de-sac she
seemed drawn by a power that could not be gainsaid.

"Julian will make for the head of the pass," she
murmured with sudden conviction. "As soon as he
escapes from the House he will come up the valley;
perhaps he has escaped already and is waiting for me
up there in the darkness. I must hurry so as not to
keep him waiting."

There was a narrow path leading into the pine-
wood, and Rosanthe turned into it without a second
thought. The moon was well up by now, shining out
of an almost cloudless sky, and enough light filtered
down through the pines to make her course easy,
however much the path twisted and turned among
the trees.

Rosanthe went on without fear—save only for the
vague dread of pursuit—though the wood through
which her way ran might well have inspired terrors
in the least sensitive heart. For there were noises in
the wood which, had she stopped to think, she could
not have explained: soft pad-padding of feet; the
scraping sound as of rough fur against rougher tree-
boles; odd animal noises, squeaks and cries, very
loud in the stillness.

But Rosanthe went forward without heeding them

now, for the thought of Julian waiting for her alone at the World's End filled her mind to the exclusion of all other things. What she was thinking about Julian she did not know, though from time to time the thought of him troubled her almost with a kind of irritation. But that did not halt her, and she still continued through the wood up an ever-steepening slope, until on a sudden she came to a clearing which seemed to be hedged all about with tall, impenetrable yew.

Directly ahead was a narrow archway cut in the hedge. Rosanthe came and stood in it, hesitating with a sudden overpowering sensation of awe, and at a loss how to proceed as another hedge seemed to shut out the way immediately ahead of her.

And suddenly a Voice spoke to her from beyond the farther hedge, a gentle full Voice which won her instant confidence:

"Do not be afraid, for I am here to lead you through the maze. Turn to the right without fear, and go forward steadily: I will accompany you on the other side of the hedge, and as we go, we can talk together, if anything troubles you that can be expressed even in the most inarticulate thoughts."

Instinctively, she did not know why, Rosanthe put her hand to her neck and felt for her necklace and cross—only to realise with a sudden pang that she had left them on the unopened book beside the bed in her room at Eclwyseg Manor.

"Let not your heart be troubled," said the Voice that was so near to her beyond the dark yew-hedge. "Julian wears your cross: he will set it about your neck when you find him at the World's End; but what that cross symbolizes he bears for you in his heart always."

They went on in silence for a little way, and then

the thought of Julian began again to trouble Rosanthe.

"You are not thinking of *his* happiness," said the Voice gently, in answer to the thought which she had not expressed consciously even to herself. "You are thinking of yourself in relation to him, not of his life in you."

"But I don't want to sink my own individuality in Julian," protested Rosanthe out loud. "I can give myself to him perfectly well, but still live my own life quite distinctly."

"That would be to live by bread alone," said the Voice. "Love receives all by giving, but you must give too, and with no thought of receiving."

Rosanthe mused upon this as she went forward ever deeper into the heart of the maze, and a new thought grew out of it.

"Why should it be give, give, give all the time? Why should we sacrifice our lives, even if Julian and I sacrifice them to each other?"

"Only if you give your life can you find it," came the answer, "and all sacrifice is of the heart."

"But sacrifice is such a big pompous word," objected Rosanthe.

"Sacrifice is always a big thing," replied the Voice, "particularly when it is smaller in compass than a grain of mustard seed."

"But what we are looking for is happiness," said Rosanthe, though rather vaguely, and conscious that she was struggling to find reasons, "and how can we find it if we go wilfully into sacrifice and repression and pain?"

"Happiness, as you call it, cannot be sought for," was the gentle answer. "It can only come to us of itself, though we may bring it to others—and once again find unconsciously in the act of giving. Give all things, and maybe you shall receive: though pain is the true joy, even as life is born out of pain, and death also is the pain of life."

These were not easy thoughts to assimilate, and Rosanthe walked on for a long time in silence, until she came suddenly to another archway in the yew hedge, and paused to look in wonder at the strange scene which was being enacted on the open plot of grass at the maze's centre.

It was a large place, with an archway leading through the hedge on the other side; and immediately in front of that farther arch, shining in the moonlight, a strange and beautiful bird was engaged in building a nest of sticks, pine cones and aromatic herbs. It moved gravely and sedately—a great bird as big as an eagle, but shaped more like a falcon, the body a deep reddish purple, its tail of azure blue intermingled with feathers of a rose carnation colour, while its neck was of shining gold, and of gold shot with shimmering blue the tall tuft of feathers which sprang from its head.

It moved with a strangely grave determination about the nest, setting all in order with its curved beak and long, shining claws. And Rosanthe watched fascinated, and with an odd and ever-growing sensation of wonder and awe. Very soon all was complete, and then the bird entered the nest and stood upright in the centre of it, with wings outstretched in an arc on either side and its head thrown back so that the tall crest gleamed behind and around it like a halo.

And suddenly it began to sing. . . . Rosanthe could never remember the nature of that song: the completion and sublimation of all music, of all birds, of all the sounds of nature, of the singing of man and woman, and of all the instruments that they have made or imagined—the harp of Apollo, the lyre of

Zethos, the pipe of Pan. In it was also the musical harmony of words, chiming in tune to the thought behind the soul of poetry; the harmony of man with nature as the heart rises in a moment of true happiness looking upon beauty, when the silence is itself a song; the symphony of communion between two whose love has passed beyond the compass of word or caress. . . . But Rosanthe recognised the music, for she had heard a dim echo of it in the room in the House of Fear, when she had seen the third figure in the mist; she had known the nature of the singing when the Voice spoke to her from behind the yew-hedge in the maze.

There were no words to the song, yet words were passing through her mind as she listened—slight, simple words which Julian had once written for her:

The distant music of your heart and mine,
That has no words nor any form of song,
Fills the mute halls of Space, and all stars shine
Within my heart that in your heart is strong.

Nor are the ages of despair in vain,
Through us the tideways of the world should part;
For love is born, and in despite of pain
Sings the eternal Phœnix in my heart.

Why she did not know, nor whence came the will to do so, but as the bird sang, Rosanthe sank slowly to her knees, and remained kneeling. The words of Julian's poem passed through her mind and into her sub-conscious recollection, but in the glory of the song a new knowledge and a new understanding seemed to grow and flourish only a little way behind her conscious perceptions, bringing with it a sense of peace and well-being far beyond her experience. Her heart sang with the Phœnix and its song grew into her heart; the tears in her eyes and the trembling of her body were the joyous pain of new life leaping and surging through her with the music.

And as these new sensations flooded over her like a blinding light and a great enlargement, the Phœnix in its nest of herbs and cedar wood began to beat its wings, faster and faster with a sound that grew from a distant murmur to a great roar; and the roar was the roar of flames long before the first curl of smoke stole up round the bird and hung in a little cloud above its head—a halo or a crown of thorns. But the flames followed the smoke in a great, leaping arch of fire: Rosanthe clasped her hands and cried out in terror or in agony; and the Phœnix cried too as it burned, cried with the pain of fire and sang with the knowledge of the new life, until it vanished in the glowing heart of the flames, and silence descended as the flames died away leaving only a little heap of glowing ashes.

"Oh, it's dead, it's dead!" sobbed Rosanthe, "and the song is ended."

"Not so," corrected the Voice from behind her, "the song is but begun and the Phœnix has passed through pain. See how it rises new and more glorious from the ashes of its own sacrifice; but now on wings new-filled with strength to bear it away over all the world to the garden by the well of life where its true home is, with voice of song that shall be heard as it passes and make glad the hearers in the joy of the joying bird."

Swiftly the glowing ashes drew together into a pyramid: taller and taller grew the gleaming mound into a slim obelisk. Then suddenly it crumbled away from the top downwards, the dust of the dead fire curling out from the main stem on either side like the arms of a cross and fluffing into a white cloud of downy ash. There was a glowing heart to the cloud; the dust grew thinner, and settled once more, leaving where it had been the shining figure of the Phœnix infinitely more bright and glorious than when Rosanthe had first seen it.

Then the song without words broke out anew as the Phœnix rose in the air, towering upon its shining wings until it seemed no bigger than the evening star. The song died into the distance, but the echo of it sang and exulted in Rosanthe's heart, bringing with it quite peace and serene determination.

"I must go to Julian," she said simply, "for we love one another, and he is seeking for me alone among the cold rocks at the World's End."

"Go forward without fear, my daughter," said the Voice behind her—so close behind that she could feel that there was no hedge between them any longer. "Go forward through the wood and up the mountain side, and the song will guide you. When you come to the top, Julian will be waiting for you, though he too must pass this way—and alone; yet shall he be there to greet you. Pass across the ashes of the Phœnix nest and by the archway in the hedge: you will not wander now from the path."

"But cannot you come with me—to show me the way?" asked Rosanthe.

"You will not go alone now," replied the Voice, a great joy sounding in the quiet words, "nor ever again. The song shall be with you in the wood. I must remain here and plant a rose-tree among the ashes, that it may grow like the Phœnix and bloom before Julian comes. Go swiftly now and seek the mystery of the World's End."

Then Rosanthe ran lightly across the little grass

plot, the ashes flying round her feet as she passed where the fire had been, and out into the wood through the arch in the tall hedge: but she did not look behind to see who had been speaking with her: she thought it was only the gardener.

The Singing Rose

For we, beside our nurse's knee,
  In fairy tales had heard
Of that strange rose which blossoms free
On boughs of an enchanted tree,
  And sings like any bird!
And of the weed beside the way
That leadeth lovers' steps astray.
            The Singing Rose: ANDREW LANG.

Julian ached still from his fall into the cellar. He had suffered no harm by it, and had been able to rise at once to his feet and follow down a rough and broken stairway the noise which came up to him from the banquet in the vault. But when the lights were struck out after his appeal to Rosanthe, and the shrieking, jostling mass of feasters surged across the table, he had not found strength enough to win through, though he leaped forward among the dishes, kicking and striking in the darkness at those who sought to stay him, and shouted out again and again to Rosanthe that he was coming to her rescue.

But her voice grew fainter and fainter in the distance, and when at last he escaped from the clutches of the dozen or so unseen hands which held him, she no longer answered his shout, and he himself was hopelessly lost among a forest of stone pillars and of low arches with which his head came into unpleasantly frequent contact. He was forced to grope his way slowly, and to trust that he was steering a comparatively straight course, while cursing himself for having failed Rosanthe in her hour of need, particularly when the chance had come immediately after a speech, the meaning of which burned strongly within him, yearning to be made good in deeds as well as in words.

And in course of time Julian came to the wall of the vault, along which he groped his way for what seemed an age, until he came to an open doorway at the foot of a spiral staircase of stone. Up this he groped until he encountered an obstacle of wood which on further investigation proved to be a door held shut by a large bolt which moved easily enough in its sockets as soon as he found it. The door then opened immediately, and Julian found himself looking once more into the great entrance hall at Eclwyseg Manor.

Without a moment's hesitation Julian stepped into the room, the door closing with a bang behind him. Looking about, he found that nothing seemed to have changed since he and Rosanthe had left it together after their strange supper: the fire still burned redly in the big grate, and he noticed a log with an odd growth on the top, which was not yet consumed, though he remembered having seen it already alight while they were sitting together on the hearthrug.

But Julian did not hesitate long in the hall: the night seemed to be calling him; the warm, stuffy atmosphere of the room to be stifling him until he longed passionately for the clean night air and the arc of stars behind the branches of trees.

He strode across the red sand-stone floor towards the door which was in deep shadow on the dark side of the room; but as he passed the foot of the stair-case leading to the upper floor, a voice called to him:

"Julian, wait a moment!"

Looking up he saw the man who had stood beside Rosanthe's chair at the subterranean banquet; the bored, sensual, over-groomed man called Phileros— "who looked rather too much like a wedding guest to be quite a gentleman," quoted Julian with relish.

Phileros sauntered down the stairs and leaned against the banisters about five steps from the bottom.

"See here, Julian," he continued in more his normal voice of bland patronage, "if you're looking for Rosanthe you haven't a chance of finding her by yourself. There are miles and miles of woods outside, with hundreds of paths winding about in each of them. . . . Why not wait here until the morning (it will surely begin to get light before long) and then we'll organise a proper search party? Look, there's plenty of wine left: let's sit comfortably by the fire and chat. I know a heap of stories, besides having a reputation, in the best circles, of course, for coining more Wildisms of the right. . . ."

But Julian cut in brusquely: "I don't agree with you. Rosanthe, if she has escaped from the House as I believe she has, will have made for the top of the valley: I *must* follow; indeed I don't want to do anything else. You can hardly expect me to stay here at such a time—even to hear the best talk and drink the best wine imaginable."

"There's nothing so unexpected as the expected when it really happens," murmured Phileros, but Julian did not stop to listen. He strode on into the shadow, up the two stone steps, and confronted the door. For a moment he was at a loss; but then he saw that it was held by a great iron latch extending more than halfway across it and raised from without by a metal lever attached to a screw passed through the centre of the knocker. He pushed up the latch and tugged at the door: it opened without difficulty, forcing him backwards down the steps, where he stood for a moment with a feeling of impendent fear as he saw a bright beam of moonlight slanting in through the porch and full on to the great iron knocker.

Nerving himself, he followed the beam to its end, and saw the wrought-iron face curling satanically about the great ring held in its jaws. But there was no horror in the face now: Julian looked at it and wondered that there had ever been. It was a strong, fierce countenance, but the only fear in it was such as the face of a lion or tiger holds for us as we see it behind the secure bars of a cage. With a great gladness Julian strode past the door, up the steps, under the porch and away into the night without ever a glance behind him.

His footsteps rang hollowly on stone paving for a moment, and were then deadened in the short grass of a well-trimmed lawn that gave like velvet to his feet. Across it he went, down a few steps from the terrace, and once more found himself on the path which led ever more steeply up the valley. Once he looked back and saw the long building of the House of Fear shining whitely between the trees; but all his thoughts were for the path before him, and as he walked he whistled softly to himself.

Up he went, winding between tall oaks at first, until these gave way to close-growing pines and groves of fir trees. He could see the tall cliffs on his right rising up only a hundred yards away from him, and the lower rocks of the hills on his left closing swiftly in to form the strange pass from which there was no egress.

And then quite unexpectedly he came to a narrow grassy ride branching away to the left, and turned into it without any thought that he had departed from the forward path. But in a little while he came out on to the open clearing in front of the high yew hedges of the maze, and paused before the archway which led into it, awe and at the same time a deadening of all anxieties coming swiftly over him.

Then the Voice spoke from behind the hedge, and Julian bent to the Voice in reverence:

"Enter in by the strait gate, for otherwise you can never come to the heart of the maze; and through the heart of it you must pass to where Rosanthe waits you at the World's End."

"I do not fear," said Julian, "but such an awe is upon me that I desire greatly to hide myself away from sight—for I am not worthy."

"Fear not," the Voice persisted. "In true awe lies joy and a great peace: only in the dread of its greatness do you find fear."

Then Julian passed through the archway and walked forward between the hedges.

"Yes," said the Voice, speaking very gently with only the black leaves of yew between them, and answering Julian's unasked question, "there is still fear in your thoughts of Rosanthe: for a true love is the strongest power in the world—stronger than the world itself—and it is hard to escape wholly from the fear of it into the serene awe of the union that is not altogether of this world."

"Is there not then any of the knowledge of my unworthiness in this fear?" asked Julian.

"The humility of that knowledge," replied the

Voice, "is divided from the pride of possessing such knowledge by so fine a razor edge that it is not good to think upon either. Give all to her: your first thoughts, your first care, your first endeavour—and forget all such fine distinctions of self-analysis. Know yourself, but know yourself in the heart of Rosanthe. Then all shall be swallowed up in the glorious moments of supremest life: and the ages of care between those moments shall be the quiet tranquillity of love and the true fulness of your lives."

Then Julian came to the heart of the maze and beheld a rose tree growing in front of the arch in the yew hedge at the opposite side of the green-sward bower, and on either side of the rose tree stood Rhoda and Rosamund clad the one in red and the other in white with robes that curved about them to the ground in one sweep, girdled with gold, without sleeves, and divided at the sides.

The rose tree showed darkly between them, the leaves grey in the dead light, the shoots and branches coral pink, and the stem dark: in the centre of the leaves grew one rose of purest white, shining like the moon among the tree-tops.

And when Julian saw the Rose he desired above all things to pluck it so that he might set it upon the breast of Rosanthe.

"It is the Singing Rose," said the Voice, "the Rose which you have sought for so long, the divine Flower of Rosanthe's love."

Then Julian stepped swiftly across the green grass towards the shadowy rose tree, but Rhoda and Rosamund barred his way with their white arms.

"Julian, do not touch the magic rose!" they cried. "It will not live when you have plucked it, but will wither at once into brown, stinking petals of decay.

Only on the tree is the Rose beautiful: admire it Julian; worship it if you will; inhale the scent of it; listen to its song, if mortal ears may hear it—but do not seek to pluck it."

Then Julian stood in doubt, and the Voice did not answer the questions in his heart—no, not when he cried out aloud:

"What shall I do? Tell me, Lord of the Garden, what shall I do?"

It was Rhoda who replied:

"Turn aside, Julian, turn aside in haste. There are other roses in the garden of the world—red roses of life that shall bloom in glory on the white breasts of love, until your lips shall crush the flowers into scent, into the fallen petals of forgetfulness."

"Come with us, Julian," said Rosamund, bending towards him until her hair brushed his cheek, "and we will lead you out of this dangerous place into a simple, comfortable bower. The roses do not sing in our abode—but how unnatural is a rose that does! Oh, come with us, Julian, and take your choice from among the many roses in the bower of youth: why set your heart upon one strange bloom that will bring you little comfort, when to do so you must forswear all the garden of roses?"

Then Julian fell upon his knees, not heeding the words of Rhoda and Rosamund, for suddenly behind their voices he heard the Rose sing. Yes, a faint music from beyond the distance and a voice out of the heart of the great white rose. He could not hear the words of the song, or if he heard them, they were lost immediately to his conscious mind. But the substance of the song remained with him, like the scent of a rose when the flower itself is withdrawn, and all memory of Rhoda and Rosamund passed from him like a dream in the dawning, so that when he looked up at the Rose he was alone. But there was no loneliness in his solitude, nor any cessation in the song of the Rose. For Rosanthe was very near to him in thought, in vivid pictures of frankly romantic character which he recognised clearly as such and rejoiced to welcome to the full thus in their rightful context. Pictures in soft, warm colours chasing one another and merging as they passed: scenes at sunset, on windy mountain slopes, in ruined castles, on tower tops high above grey cities; scenes in an ancient red-walled garden, by the fireside at home, in place after place that was dearly associated with his childhood: but always Rosanthe was with him, was very near to him, near until the world was lost in her eyes—and all was hers now and dear to her as it was dear to him.

Then, still kneeling, he stretched out his hand to the Rose and sought to pluck it: but the tough stem defied every effort, and the sharp thorns drove back all his attempts.

Then the Voice spoke just behind Julian, quietly, reassuringly:

"No mortal hand may pluck the Singing Rose, nor can it be the possession of one alone."

"But I seek only to gather it for Rosanthe," cried Julian, "this, the divine flower of her love and mine."

"Her love and yours," repeated the Voice. "Even so. The Singing Rose in your heart and in hers, whence neither you nor she may pluck it. Yet it is one Rose, and it shall be gathered. But go forth now, Julian, from the Garden of this Rose, and seek the Garden of the Rose of your heart. Follow where the song shall lead, for Rosanthe awaits you at the World's End."

Then Julian arose and walked with bent head past the Singing Rose, through the archway in the yew hedge, and out into the dark wood. But he did not look behind him, for he knew Who was the Gardener.

To the World's End

> ... Sun and wind and flowers and birds
> In language deeper drawn than human words,
> From deeper founts than Time shall e'er destroy,
> All spoken to thee. ...
>   *The Coming of Love:* T. WATTS-DUNTON.

Walking in the dense wood by different paths, Julian and Rosanthe drew nearer and nearer to one another as they came up the valley. The cliffs closed in upon either side, higher and more forbidding at every step; the trees grew scanter and scanter—little more than a strip twenty yards wide up the middle of the pass where an unseen stream clattered down among the rocks with a gurgling music of laughter and lament.

Turning to look back in the brilliant moonlight they found themselves gazing through a mighty gateway into the open world outside: they were walking out of the world into the unknown darkness where the sides of the pass met, but behind them all the Kingdoms seemed to be spread out in a great panorama reaching to the distant hills on the horizon.

They shivered as they looked—standing within

speaking distance of one another, though neither knew it—but the night was warm, with a balmy breath of full summer in the air, and any chill came from within.

But there was no thought of turning back. After the one glance round the wide expanse of valley and mountain, of open field and wooded glade, both turned once more and continued on their way up the narrow paths on either side of the rift in the rocks through which flowed the stream.

Was there a voice singing at the top of the pass, a music beyond the distance and behind the darkness? Or was it but the soft breeze of a midsummer night whispering among the pine trees on the lofty skyline in front of them, and echoing the music in their own hearts? Neither could tell, nor indeed did either pause to wonder; but they walked on as if in a dream, looking straight ahead, even when the trees thinned about them and ceased, leaving only a narrow grassy glade in the heart of the mountain.

A turn of the paths led them towards one another and brought them suddenly to a narrow stream of leaping silver light and iron shadow which murmured across the open grass to lose itself among the trees and rocks below. And when the stream stopped them, each looked and found the other standing not two feet away: and at first they spoke only the other's name, though with more meaning in the names than in a mountain of epithets:

"Rosanthe!"

"Julian!"

But the stream was between them still, and they went forward hand in hand, walking on either side of it and speaking no other word, for all had been said, though much remained to be spoken.

And in a little while they came to the very head of

the pass, where the grassy slope curved round in front of them to bar their way, with cliffs and scattered trees rising behind and above the slope. And there the stream had its source, bubbling out beneath the roots of a tall and ancient tree, an evergreen oak with great leaves and spreading branches shadowing all behind it, though in front the moonlight filled the place with radiance right up to its foot.

Between the tree and the spot where the stream welled up was a little flat space made of twisted roots lightly soiled over with a matting of leaves and tendrils out of which grew thick short grass: and here Julian and Rosanthe met, coming together very slowly until their arms were about one another and their lips were joined in a long kiss.

At last they drew apart, but only to arms' length, and stood thus, still holding the one to the other, but looking each into the other's face with a long, searching gaze. And presently they were aware of music once more, near to them, yet beyond all distance, growing out of the silence and clinging about them like the breath of the warm night breeze.

Looking out through the gateway of the cliffs and across the wide expanse of valley, they saw a meteor shoot down towards them out of the distant sky, and knew that it was the Phœnix returning towards the earth. Then they clung together once more, in the wonder of the bird's approach, and saw it settle in the dark tree above them where it shone and glimmered so brightly that they might not look at it for long.

Yet during the instant sight they saw that it held in its golden beak a great white Rose; and as they let fall their eyes and drew together once more, the Rose fell with a murmur of song and lay upon Rosanthe's bosom for a moment, resting on the lyre-shaped brooch between her breasts as if it had been pinned there. She felt the cool caress of the petals like the reverent kiss of the supreme pledge, and the scent and the song were about them both, clouding their eyes and dimming their senses with the uttermost peace.

And as they stood there with only the Rose between them, the music and the song swelled and murmured about them into a deep harmonious triumph of words of age-old meaning, well known to them and yet that instant created:

> Here in the shadow of man's knowing,
>> Beyond the shades eternally,
> And through the world, a bright shape going,
>> Still in your heart the heart of me.
>
> Here in the world to eyes scarce seeing,
>> Hid and revealed in your desire,
> Ghost of the peace that still is fleeing
>> Eternal fledgeling of the fire.
>
> Here in the heart for ever dwelling,
>> Lost in the heart that seeks me there;
> Flesh of your flesh by flesh compelling;
>> Yet must Ixion clasp the air.
>
> Here in your form my form completing,
>> Your subject and your deity,
> Still through the world a bright shape fleeting,
>> Found in your heart the heart of me.

The music died away into the silence of the night; the Phœnix was gone from the tree; and there was no Rose in the brooch at Rosanthe's breast. But as they passed together into the little cave behind the tree at the World's End, they seemed to hear the song of

the Phœnix, of the Rose, of the Voice, singing beyond
the distance and behind the night—still in their hearts
that sang with the joy of a great understanding and of
a greater peace.

And, too tired for word or wonder, they lay down
upon the soft sandy floor, and entered immediately
into a deep and dreamless sleep.

The sun rose beyond the World's End and was
shining down the pass and out across the valley before Julian and Rosanthe woke.

For a little while they lay without word or movement, conscious only of a supreme sense of happiness
and well-being, Julian curled up against the wall of
the cave, and Rosanthe lying across the little sandy
floor with her head pillowed on his shoulder.

"Rosanthe," murmured Julian at last, his breath
stirring her hair, "Rosanthe! Are you awake?"

"Yes, Julian," she answered, sitting up slowly,
"I've just woken up. But where on earth are we?"

"It's a cave—unless we are still dreaming," he
said, rubbing his eyes. "And look! the sun's shining
outside."

"A cave . . . the sun shining . . ." Rosanthe rose
slowly to her feet, as did Julian also, and they stood
a little way apart in the centre of the cave. Then with
a quick movement she took his hand, and they went
out into morning and stood beneath the tree with the
stream bubbling out at their feet like the Fountain of
Life in the Earthly Paradise on the world's eastern
verge.

They looked out over the tree tops, between the
great cliffs, and across the wide valley which shone
green and silver in the sweet freshness of a new day.

"This must be the World's End," said Julian after
a long pause, "the top of the pass above Eclwyseg

which the old boy at Dinas Bran was talking about. Rosanthe, it is the World's End indeed, isn't it?"

"No, Julian," she answered with a little thrill in her voice, "it's the World's Beginning. . . . Come out into the world with me, Julian, for the world lies all before us. . . ."

He turned slowly towards her, and she came to him with a little catch in her breath as she spoke his name; with a quick movement he held her to him, murmuring "my darling," and their lips met.

Presently they went down the pass together, hand in hand; between the tall cliffs, and out into the world once more. They walked in silence for a long time, but at length Rosanthe said:

"Julian; about last night. . . . I had a whole series of the oddest and most vivid dreams—and how did we come to that cave?"

"I was wondering that," answered Julian, also very thoughtful. "We came to the old house—Eclwyseg Manor—together, when my car broke down; all well and good. But then the odd things began to happen, and I only remember them until we woke up this morning in the cave."

"Odd things?" queried Rosanthe. "Tell me about them, Julian."

"I can't remember very clearly," he answered. "There was an inscription on the house in Welsh saying 'Let him who has no fear, fear here'—that's clear enough—and a feeling of terror as we stood in the porch. But after that, all is blurred and indistinct. There was a lighted hall; a strange meal—two strange meals, only the second was in some sort of vault and there were lots of people besides ourselves. And then a hideous jumble of faces, and passions and impulses, and a great oppression—until I seemed to win out into the night."

"Yes," broke in Rosanthe, "and shadows in the mist; a pageant in which I took part; until I also escaped from the house. Then there was the Phœnix —the maze; the Gardener; and you and I meeting outside the cave. . . ."

"And the Singing Rose," interrupted Julian excitedly, "and the song. The Phœnix sat on the tree above the spring—just as in the old legends—only it dropped the Singing Rose into our hearts. . . . Rosanthe, where does waking end and dreaming begin?"

"We are awake now," she said with decision, and they paused for a moment in the middle of the path to kiss—much to the amazement of a little red squirrel which popped out of a hole in an oak tree just ahead of them, and sat up on its hind legs with quivering tail and a nut held half-way to its mouth.

They went out in silence and came suddenly to the grassy clearing in front of Eclwyseg Manor. Slowly, almost with awe, they walked up the stone steps and on to the smoothly mown terrace in front of it.

"I thought the house was much bigger," murmured Rosanthe, "with dozens of windows instead of those three or four either side of the door."

They stopped in front of it and Julian read out in a hushed voice the inscription: "Ovner na wyr ovn', 'Let him who has no fear, fear here'. So that was genuine," he said. "And there's another plaque with a list of the names of ancient Kings of Wales whose descendants lived in this house after Dinas Bran was destroyed. I'm supposed to be descended from one of them—but I don't know."

"Well, there's nothing inside the house now," said Rosanthe, peering in through one of the dusty diamond panes. "Only bare floors and the plaster dropping from the walls. . . . Come along, Julian, we ought to hurry, particularly if we have to walk all the way to the main road to find someone to mend your car."

So they set off once more down the narrow road, and before long came to the abandoned car. Julian eyed it with resignation, and remarked valiantly:

"I'll just have one tinker at it—for luck, you know, darling." He seated himself first in the driving seat, however, and after surveying the dashboard for a few moments, pressed the self-starter thoughtfully—and immediately the engine purred, spluttered and roared into life.

"It's actually working!" he exclaimed in triumph. "I can't *think* what was wrong with it yesterday!"

Rosanthe sprang in beside him, laughing mischievously at his bewilderment:

"You'd better learn something about cars, Julian, before you take me driving again! But hurry up now, or my grandmother will be hiring detectives. She probably suspects the worst as it is!"

"Let her suspect," smiled Julian, "grandmothers always do—they just adore it."

"She'll ask your intentions," said Rosanthe gravely, "and then begin fixing a date for the wedding."

"Do you like dates?" asked Julian inconsequently.

"Some dates," Rosanthe answered with studied indifference, "particularly dates next spring. . . . Look out, Julian, you'll run into the wall if you try to kiss me while you're driving! . . . Why, Julian—how long have you been wearing my chain and cross?"

"Since last night," he answered. And after that there were no more words to speak.

The car turned out of the narrow lane and was speedily lost among the steady stream of traffic.

THE WORLD'S BEST
ADULT FANTASY

from Ballantine Books

THE CHILDREN OF LLYR
Evangeline Walton $.95

THE CREAM OF THE JEST
James Branch Cabell $1.25

NEW WORLDS FOR OLD
Edited by Lin Carter $1.25

SPAWN OF CTHULHU
H. P. Lovecraft and Others $.95

THE MAN WHO WAS THURSDAY
G. K. Chesterton $.95

VATHEK   William Beckford $.95

DOUBLE PHOENIX   Edmund Cooper
and Roger Lancelyn Green $1.25

WATER OF THE WONDROUS ISLES
William Morris $1.25

KHALED   F. Marion Crawford $1.25

THE WORLD'S DESIRE
H. Rider Haggard and Andrew Lang $1.25

AND MORE! Send for full catalog

To order by mail, send price of book plus 10¢ for
mailing to Dept. CS, Ballantine Books, 36 West
20th Street, New York, N.Y. 10003